An Awareness of March

SCEPTRE

Also by Alison Dye

The Sense of Things
Memories of Snow

An Awareness of March

ALISON DYE

SCEPTRE

First published in 1997 by Hodder and Stoughton
A division of Hodder Headline PLC
A Sceptre Book

10 9 8 7 6 5 4 3 2 1

British Library Cataloguing in Publication Data

Dye, Alison
An Awareness of March
1. English fiction – 20th century
I. Title
823.9'14 [F]

ISBN 0 340 65390 6

Typeset by Palimpsest Book Production Limited,
Polmont, Stirlingshire
Printed and bound in Great Britain by
Mackays of Chatham PLC, Chatham, Kent

Hodder and Stoughton
A division of Hodder Headline PLC
338 Euston Road
London NW1 3BH

For Rita McCarthy

1 S

Jackie Molloy, aged sixty, is walking down Ninth Avenue. South from 48th Street to the corner of 44th, his twenty-four-hour launderette.

Two a.m., Monday, 14 March 1994. Thirty-five years to the day.

He prefers the darkness. He does not shrink from shadows or blackened alleys, nor does he startle at disembodied sounds made by furtive creatures that pillage in obscurity. Clatter and echo of bins, the rape of bins, hissing, snarling, and scurrying.

Jackie prefers the shading of light, the softening of glare. He is not safe in the harsh exposure of mornings, he slinks away and dies at the daily expectation that he waken. That he drag his mind past mountains of tangibles along hours of light. His eyes and his skin would leak, slashed from such an assault of light. Two a.m., Monday, 14 March 1994, Jackie Molloy is wearing sunglasses against the most microscopic shard of daytime.

He is pulling a cart. In the cart is a faded white pillowcase stuffed with clothes and towels needing their weekly wash. He gently tips the cart and pulls it at a comfortable angle. Appreciates the click-click of the rickety wheels as they encounter and pass over the seams in the footpath. One bag of laundry could be carried, but Jackie would miss the companionship of his cart, its gentle wobble like a nuzzle, the satisfaction of a smooth pull, the negotiation around rifts and crevices, the deftness of the yank up each curb and into the straightaway, up each curb and into the straightaway.

On the bars of the cart Jackie has looped rubber bands, tied bits of string, and taped laundry and grocery receipts. A tiny calendar from the liquor store. He might drape special items of clothing whose care he needs to discuss with Miguelito, the young son of the owner of the laundromat. The cart is Jackie's filing cabinet, his office, his desk. And when Jackie speaks to it and strokes it, to apologise for a heavy load or a bad bump, the cart is his warm and loyal pet accompanying him unconditionally on his cautious excursions.

This night, this early morning, only hours away now from the dawn of the day on which it happened and was discovered, Jackie is stooped. He will survive this anniversary, like all the others, by putting his head down and down, until he is lowered into a shallow grave. Where he disguises himself as ashes against the deafening pestilence. Its yearly buzzing and beating of wings, demanding the sacrifice. Until at last, one minute past twelve, 15 March, failing to discover the burnt and buried offering, the locusts will move on to await next year's search. Jackie knows how to do this disappearance, and 1994 will be no different, perhaps even easier than other years. For this year his body has entered old age. Jackie Molloy, the mind sodden, the spirit drained, is imagining his way into extinction. At last I am an old man, soon I will be over. As he and his cart move slowly through the litter on the footpath. Bags, wrappers and containers, bodies and bottles.

His friend Martinez is having a seizure, and the needle standing in his arm shivers. Jackie weaves respectfully around him. Leave a man in peace in his own living room. Inviolable invisible lines drawn on the footpath, not to cross the threshold of privacy.

Jackie is mostly grey now. His hair flops at an angle across his forehead, still thick but no longer black, no longer gleaming. His old khakis are baggy, the paunch that used to hang over the belt is gone. He drank a lot in the early days but not now. Alcohol is no use. A failure at the big questions, a cheat on the small ones, nothing but broken promises from booze. He stops outside Miguelito's and adjusts the sunglasses.

Miguelito lights the launderette with three bare bulbs and this particular day of all days Jackie will need filters for what will threaten to pass through obscurity into day. He has seen the calendar, the date that does not lie. The yearly peeling away of skin.

Ah, Senor Molloy, how you are tonight? Give to me, you hurt you back pulling and pulling your little baby. Hello, baby, you park yourself right over here while I do your daddy's laundry – I do it for you tonight, Molloy, no extra charge. You looking bad in the dumps.

Down in the dumps.

Bad, down, hey Molloy, I give you nice offer so shut up with your big words. Sit over there by your baby. Coffee, Molloy? Gin?

Coffee.

Miguelito walks past the row of washing machines grinding, churning, bubbling, the dryers spinning billows of white and red and blue and orange, a soft warm garden, and Jackie is transported by the tumbling of these puffs. He holds the handle of his cart, is drawn into the dryer and lost. Suddenly Miguelito is beside him.

Hey, you at a seance, Molloy? Drink the coffee, wake you up.

I don't want to wake up, thinks Jackie, don't want.

Miguelito kisses Jackie on the cheek and runs a hand through his hair.

You a real gentleman, Molloy, look at that nice grey hair. I'm telling you, we be good together, you think it over, like I always say, maybe someday you kiss me back, and wowee, I go to the moon that day.

Miguelito draws away, leaving Jackie with the coffee. He blows Jackie a kiss.

I wait for you, Molloy, good things is worth the wait. Now I wash your clothes.

Are, Miguelito, mumbles Jackie. *Are* worth the wait.

Molloy, honey, I got a piece advice for you: kiss more, talk less, you be happy man. You want powder or liquid?

Jackie cannot answer, he is transported again to the kaleidoscope of clothes buffeting about in the dryer. He holds the coffee. The heat from the cup comforts him.

Okay, so powder then. I got more powder than liquid.

Miguelito busies himself loading and unloading the machines, transferring mounds of wet clothing into dryers, bouncing dry things into plastic baskets that sit beneath the door of each machine. The clips on the doors rattle and bang as Miguelito makes his rounds whistling and singing softly to himself, nudging doors open and closed with his foot, moving easily along the rows like a skater. He lifts the baskets of dry clothes one at a time on to the table in the centre of the shop where he sorts and folds, his fingers moving back and forth across the table as if a piano.

And then, then. Jackie is disturbed by something, no one can say what, the day, the night, and without explanation, as if an irrestible nugget has been put before his eyes, he looks out of Miguelito's big window on to Ninth Avenue.

Standing at the corner is a man eating a slice of pizza. The pizza parlour across the street from the launderette stays open until four a.m. The man is struggling with the pizza, cheese is dripping, he is trying to catch it in his mouth. He is holding up the slice and strings of cheese dangle in too many directions for him to get them all in his mouth at once, so he starts taking quick bites. Jackie stands up. He takes off his sunglasses and squints.

What you see there, Molloy? Huh? Somebody you know?

Jackie watches the man. He has finished the pizza. Under the streetlight he pulls a napkin from his pocket. He is wearing an expensive suit and tie, horn-rimmed glasses, an overcoat that must be cashmere, and carrying a leather satchel. His hair is neat, closely trimmed. He is respectable, well-to-do, at home with himself. Without splits or contradictions. He lifts his chin into the light and wipes his mouth.

Jackie comes alive. Elation on 14 March? Impossible. He no longer has such experiences, on any day, of light and sun. But there is no denying that the vision of grown-up Bobby Wilmot has penetrated one small encrusted window in the tomb, and awakened Jackie Molloy.

He keeps looking. Oh God in Heaven, can it be true? It *is* true, there is the proof, there is Bobby Wilmot, a fine young man. All hope was not lost. All goodness, integrity, and honesty were not smeared with waste, possibility not smashed like eggs. Bobby Wilmot has emerged intact from that soiled time of degradation thirty-five years to the day. A descendant in whom appearance at last matches reality, double dirty lives cleansed, become one.

So Jackie was wrong: this anniversary will not repeat all others, will not repeat the story. Jackie Molloy will be able to dissolve into nothingness in peace. Redeemed through Bobby's escape.

Jackie moves closer to the window. He cannot feel his feet touch the floor, he is floating. Unplanned, unplanned, what happened to the plan? He stares. The man senses someone looking at him. He turns toward the launderette, toward Jackie standing in the window. His eyes and Jackie's meet, it is always in the eyes. Then the man drops his napkin in a bin and begins to walk off. Jackie moves toward the door.

Hey – where you going, Molloy? You okay?

Still floating, Jackie leaves the laundromat, leaves the sunglasses, and begins to follow the vision of Bobby Wilmot. Oh God, please not another mirage, please let it be water.

Up Ninth Avenue. Jackie believes the man is going to a tower of expensive condominium apartments two blocks away. Where he probably lives. After working late. Partner in a Wall Street law firm? Just returned from the London office?

Jackie watches the confident stride of this man. Bobby Wilmot. Strong, muscular back. New York Athletic Club. Privilege. He is not afraid of being mugged, he is at ease in the neighbourhood.

Jackie feels as though he has reached Bethlehem. He could fall on his knees and cry out with gratitude, the journey is over, the hallowed place of forgiveness is in sight. Following, following. How many years since he watched in hiding? How many years since the lost hope of reparation which comes to him now?

Until the perfect man in Jackie's perfect vision enters an unexpected place. Not the gleaming tower, not the oasis.

No. Jackie's salvation disappears into a seedy bar.

Never mind, doesn't mean anything, he probably just wants a quick drink before heading home.

But you know otherwise, Jackie Molloy, you know this neighbourhood in which the grown-up Bobby Wilmot is so comfortable. For this is not just a bar. How many more years can you keep lying to yourself about what this story has left behind?

The door your Bobby Wilmot has knocked upon, the door that has been opened to him, the threshold he has crossed, leads to a club for transvestites. The satchel holds the trappings of the secret life.

Jackie sags. He holds the cold steel pole of the streetlight. Presses his cheek against it to feel the uncompromising chill, its complete clarity and integrity an antidote to the deception of suits. Hugging the metal, he slips to the pavement, desperate to incorporate the pole. Instead, like the illusion embodied in Bobby Wilmot, it slips through Jackie's grasp. Again and again the dissolution of hopes and possibilities, the seduction of appearance.

Jackie rises and walks in slow motion, one step, stop, one step, stop, back to Miguelito's.

The ashen face appears inside the door of the little shop. Miguelito runs to Jackie and catches him before he falls. When he has settled his old friend into the chair beside his cart, he carefully replaces the dark glasses.

2

The rain comes down in grimy thicknesses and clings. Not a crisp, bright rain that might clarify, or wash remnants and residues away, but a dank liquid bearing waste.

Travelling through the blackness that hangs over New York like a vulture and reaching earth against a backdrop of tenements, rain in Hell's Kitchen is a curtain of soot draped in lethargic folds over the crumbling streets and avenues. It seeps through rotted window frames and cracked glass into rooms where people are trying to live, and traps them in bed under their coats.

Outdoors, the rain slops one piece of filth into another, clogging drains and alleys with sticky wads of detritus and spreading the wads like paste. Rats sniff and forage, catch their toes in the mush, and track disease into and out of apartments and cellars. Concrete slabs of footpaths entombing the soil of former times are spattered with brownish greyish merging and dissolution of scraps. One layer of leavings upon another, the vapours of ghosts.

This is where Jackie Molloy lives. The same furnished room he had in 1959 when he worked at the *Mirror* and the girl from 38th and Lexington was strangled. Where he found out about the story in the first place, before it was a story, from Frank who lived down the hall.

And where he returns after he believes he has seen the grown-up Bobby Wilmot.

3

Frank who lived down the hall. Who should have been and gone, no meaning or consequence to the sordid act-ings out.

Frank and his girlfriend Joanne, who let Jackie see every-thing they liked to do to each other. Who gave Jackie leads on the private stories he couldn't resist. Couples to follow and watch.

Jackie Molloy's double life. Jackie Molloy's secrets.

Frank and Joanne owned him. His salary, and hours of overtime, evaporated into their bribes. Months of payments in 1958 and early 1959 for Sarah and David Mulligan whom Frank met as a driver hired by David's public rela-tions firm. Frank let Jackie substitute for him on night duty when the Mulligans had to attend dinners and ben-efits. Sarah was struggling to be a painter, so occasionally there were openings at galleries, receptions in museums. In return, Frank demanded his lost wages plus a hun-dred dollars a month. Hey, a junkie's got to have his fix, right, Molloy? And the supplier's got to be paid. Simple economics.

One evening Jackie collected Sarah and David outside their apartment on Park Avenue and drove them to a dinner at the Waldorf-Astoria. Frank had had the car fitted with special mirrors on the dash that gave Jackie a full view of the back seat – for security purposes, the Mulligans were told – and he loaned Jackie the official cap and jacket.

Jackie was completely at peace driving the Mulligans: in the presence of his passengers, he did not have to exist. The Mulligans spoke to each other as if they were alone. They never addressed Jackie except to tell him where to go, and there was no need for Jackie to reply. In this role he was not a person. He could watch and listen as if he were invisible, entering their lives like a vapour. He waited long hours in the car for them to emerge from whatever engagement they were attending, and in these hours Jackie spoke to no one. Just lay his head back and rested in the comfort and safety of the car's containment.

On the way to the Waldorf dinner, the Mulligans did not talk. David studied notes written on small index cards: he was going to give a speech. Sarah stared out of the window. But when they returned to the car at the end of the evening, Sarah was drunk. Jackie opened the back door and David shoved her in. He then rammed himself into the front seat beside Jackie. On the ride up Park Avenue, Sarah imitated the partners in David's firm with exaggerated gestures and pomposity until she passed out. David seethed.

At their building he got out, opened the back door, and said, without looking at Jackie, Driver, will you please help me get my wife upstairs.

Where, unnoticed by David who was consumed with rage, Jackie watched him slap Sarah and force himself inside her. While their infant daughter and housekeeper slept in another room. Finally Jackie left the apartment unnoticed. Surprised that he did not feel aroused. Only cold. And went to Frank and Joanne to pay, and to feel something. Don't worry, Molloy, we won't tell anybody. Wouldn't want the big boss Marty to hear that the up-and-coming journalist of 1958 has a strange hobby, would we, Joanne? We'd hate for you to mess up a promising career.

As Joanne spreads her legs again, Jackie's reward after the payment.

And Frank holds his erection high for Jackie to see, the Washington Monument Joanne calls it. He pumps himself in time with Jackie, waits until just the right moment, digs into Joanne, in, in, eyes never leaving Jackie, brings it out to show Jackie again, then in and in again, and when it is time Joanne calls to Jackie the way Jackie likes. Frank and Joanne know his timing.

Eventually Frank lost the driving job and Jackie had to follow the Mulligans on foot. But by early 1959 they had moved out of town.

And then Jackie's timing went all wrong.

4

1954. Jackie Molly is twenty.

In the grave set of his ebony eyes, the coarse, sturdy face, the shock of black hair at a distinguished angle across his forehead and already greying at the temples, he is an old man.

Cleft chin, two rifts between his eyebrows, the serious way he conducts his slightly stooped body. He is walking east on 42nd Street, has just crossed Lexington heading toward Third. He is wearing khakis and an open-neck white shirt. No colour. No way to notice.

In the warm April breeze his hair flutters. The softness of hair wafting, brushing skin Jackie cannot feel. No allowance for this tenderness, the hair attempting to comfort. He does not walk, Jackie Molloy is not taking a walk. He anchors each step to the pavement, unflinching, unyielding shoes. He is trying to mask, but cannot, the caution. He is betrayed by his hands. It is in the hands in the pockets. The contradiction between hands and feet. The feet moving the body forward, the hands holding back.

The footpath is not crowded at eleven in the morning, but as always Jackie defines his physical boundaries like a statue. He steps deftly away from contact with passers-by, away from touch. In his moving stillness, he creates no disturbance of air, commits no violation of space. From their dark recesses his eyes search out and penetrate shifts of intention, gestures from the outside contemplating entrance. The eyes do not turn or seem to look, but draw in, draw in, and master.

A woman is holding her child's hand. Leaning down to reprimand, you may not have, you may not do, you have been told, and she is unaware of the clutches of people coming towards her. Jackie eases out of her way, all of a piece. As if he is packed in a container and can be tipped and shifted as the space demands. The way statues are crated and shipped.

Jackie has just crossed Lexington going toward Third. The *Mirror* building is on the south side. He pauses outside the imposing gold and glass doors, unfolds his newspaper and re-reads. Folds again, tucks it under his left arm, puts both hands back in his pockets. He is about to go through.

But no. He is turning away. Cannot take the step. Cannot release his right hand to reach. The pocket is warm and dark, the hand is safe. He faces the building again. A man in an expensive suit walks briskly past, takes the handle and pulls open the door. He looks back at Jackie, stands to the side. This man is holding the door, waiting for Jackie to pass through. He nods.

Jackie returns the nod and strides in ahead of this man. His sinewy legs suddenly atrophy, dangling threads. But his torso propels them forward. An appearance of poise. The feet know how to direct themselves and dominate the cowardly hands. The man in the suit believes Jackie works in this building, and he and Jackie enter the elevator together.

The man gestures to the panel of buttons.

Jackie replies: Eleven.

Several other passengers call out their destinations or press a button. The man himself is going to the eighth floor. He alights there in silence.

Eleven. *Mirror* Employment Office. Jackie walks straight

from the elevator to a woman behind a counter marked Reception.

I'm here about the ad for a reporter.

You're kidding.

No.

The woman is chewing gum. Props her chin on the heel of her hand and continues to chomp, the bone of her chin against the bone of her hand. The chin is pushing down, or the hand is pushing up. One or the other or both.

That was three weeks ago, hon. The interviews are closed.

I was away.

Come on, you can do better than that. The only place that doesn't sell the *Mirror* is Outer Mongolia. You could have phoned. Besides, they want somebody young. Somebody they can train. Sorry.

It said no experience. I don't have experience. And I'm twenty.

Yeah, sure you are. I suppose you can you read and write, too.

Yes.

The woman eyes Jackie.

That's the only thing – you gotta be able to read and write. You got a high school diploma?

Yes.

Name?

John Molloy.

Have a seat. I'll see what I can do.

Thank you.

Just so you know, you didn't have to lie about your age. I was going to get you in anyway. And you better not be lying about the high school diploma because I'm not supposed to do this when they tell me the interviews are closed. They had a lot of people in here saying they graduated high school when they didn't.

The woman leaves the counter.

Jackie sits. The paper remains under his arm, his hands in his pockets. The paper is worn from being opened, folded, and opened, for three weeks.

The woman returns to her post and a man emerges from a door behind her.

Molloy?

Yes.

This way.

Jackie enters a colourless room with no windows. A grey metal desk, two chairs. Jackie and the interviewer sit on opposite sides of the desk. The man sighs and clasps his hands across his stomach.

I got one question, Mr Molloy, and I want your answer brief. No big speeches, no philosophy. Why do you want to be a reporter?

I like to see what's going on.

That's a new one. You don't want to be the next Edward R. Murrow? Make your name in television? Be a big star? Cover the White House for NBC?

I don't have a television.

You been working?

Docks.

Who for?

Different people. Nobody in particular.

So you don't like that question. How long you down there?

A few years.

Probably got in through your father, is that it?

Maybe.

I thought so. Then how come you're looking for a job? Sounds like you got a job already.

My father's been sick.

What's the matter with him?

Emphysema. Cirrhosis.

How old?

Sixty.

Who's going to take care of him if I hire you?

He died.

Oh. Sorry. Say – that wouldn't be Mick Molloy we're talking about, would it?

Yes.

I see. So that's who your father is. Well, you could stay in with his pals, you know, be fixed for life. Longshoremen look after their own. Especially any son of the infamous Mick Molloy.

I don't want to.

Why not?

Different reasons.

You don't like that question either. Anybody ever tell you, Molloy, when you go for a job interview you're supposed to answer the questions?

No. I never heard that.

Been in the Army? Korea?

No.

Why not?

Didn't get drafted.

Oh. I see. Your father knew somebody. I'm learning how to read you, Molloy. And while we're on the subject. Another thing about interviews: don't lie about your age.

I didn't.

You got a birth certificate?

Not with me.

But you got one?

Yes.

And you know the alphabet more or less?

More or less.

Okay. Look. What happened is we never filled the job. Everybody's either in the Army or stupid. So you start Monday, City Desk. They'll put you with a guy called Marty, you follow him around, see what he does. The receptionist will give you a form on your way out, bring it back Monday. $21.50 a week, payday Friday. Any questions?

No.

Fine. There's the door, Molloy. Good luck.

5

Doors. Jackie Molloy, five years old, stays with his father in tenements near the docks. With his mother in two rooms at the back of a diner on Tenth Avenue. She is a waitress. Jackie spends many hours in a booth near the glass door of the diner. Watching the opening and closing, the entering, departing. With no idea why he suddenly goes from one place to another.

Each move is like the jolt of alarms. Shots of panic, emergency, day or night, grabbed by strange men and women. Shouting, chaos, go, get out, through doors. Open, close, corridors, alleys, lock, unlock, be quiet.

All the doors have holes for peeking out. Jackie's mother does not live with his father, Jackie's father goes to meetings, and he runs away and hides behind the doors with the holes and looks out of the tiny holes with his eye, he can see out but no one can see in, the Communists, the Government, Negroes trying to take work from the Irish. So the International Longshoremen's Association has to run away from them or else beat them up first.

So Jackie goes in and out of doors and secret rooms. He is very quiet, he is allowed to listen carefully and to watch, but may not speak or play, or the Communists and the Government will find the secret doors to the secret rooms and beat Jackie and the others up and maybe cut them with knives.

At the diner Jackie is quiet, too. He sits in his booth by the door with Cokes and hamburgers. His mother sits opposite when she has a break, gazing out of the window. Windows are like doors, the coming and going of light, and Jackie's mother wants what the window can give. She often cries, looking out from it. Jackie notices that before the tears dry and stain her cheeks, they dance in the light. Jackie watches the tears transform from sparkling glass beads to dry stains streaked with black make-up.

Sometimes on breaks Jackie's mother leaves the diner and stands on Tenth Avenue. She stares uptown and downtown, chooses one or the other, and walks. Then she comes back, hands Jackie another Coke, and takes people's orders. Jackie rests his head on the table, other women sit with him, take him for strolls and ice-creams, and put him to bed in the back of the diner.

Where he waits for his mother to open the door. To come in. To stay. Or open, come in, go. Sometimes his father comes in, lies on the bed on top of his mother, and goes.

Jackie Molloy is patient. He studies both sides of the door, how it pulls in and pushes out. All the coming and going. The closing and what is kept inside, the opening and what leaves.

And the door becomes real. Alive. Jackie's friend or enemy. With magic Jackie can make it close or make it open.

And make his mother reappear even after she has gone out of the door for good.

6

The laundry is washed, dried, folded. Miguelito has packed the items neatly and carefully in the pillowcase. This, too, is clean now, and the young man has placed a plastic bag at the bottom of the cart so the pillowcase will not get dirty on the journey home. It is four thirty. The sun not nearly up.

Jackie has had to sit a long time. Trying to steady himself from the shock. His nerves are split at the ends, sticking out in all directions, electrocuted. Crackling burning memory flew along the nerves and exploded out the ends. Remnants hang from each frazzled tip.

Big heavy ledgers have suddenly been dumped on to Jackie's lap, pinning him to Miguelito's plastic chair. He has had a look in those books in the life of the young Bobby Wilmot grown old, and he is weighed down by pages and pages of what is written there. Words and deeds and words and deeds, column after column, the accounts payable, in those ledgers the sight of Bobby, the fate of Bobby.

Miguelito has given Jackie cups of herbal tea, rosehips and hibiscus flowers. He has also turned off two of the three lightbulbs and lit a stick of jasmine incense.

I walk you home, Molloy? I serious – I lock up and walk you home, no problem. I mean it. You got to be careful.

I feel better.

You don't look better. I worried.

Jackie watches Miguelito. Trim, lithe, a sprite. He is wearing tight black jeans, a black T-shirt with curved white lines decorating the front: two dancers. On the back, New York City Ballet. Close-cropped black hair, olive skin, one small gold earring.

Help me up.

Take this arm, I got a good strong arm for you. Go slow. Okay? I open the door.

Miguelito walks delicately to the front of the shop. Jackie is weak, but standing. His eyes float in the soft space the young man has created, the rarified air above dread. He closes his eyes and sways his face from side to side, surrendering to the caress of the jasmine.

Miguelito returns. Studies Jackie through the dark lenses.

My beautiful Molloy. Something come in to you from the past.

Jackie cannot reply. The past of which Miguelito speaks is now the present. Wires are crossed, circuits burning, sirens screaming.

You got to get rid of it, Molloy. That past, it is putting poison in you blood and that poison blood is rushing everywhere through you body, you soul, man, it will sweep you away.

Miguelito pushes through the air with his arm.

You see what I mean, Molloy?

I have to sleep.

No. You got to wake up. You got to see what's happening. I don't know you secret, Molloy. But I know what it is doing to you.

It couldn't have been him.

Miguelito shakes his head.

That guy is real, Molloy.

I'll be all right tomorrow, I just have to get through today.

Miguelito winds the green plastic stem of a plastic rose around one of the bars of Jackie's cart and helps his friend outside.

7

Back in his room. Five a.m.

Jackie takes off his sunglasses. He parks his cart in the space between his low fridge and the sink. He hauls the pillowcase out and plunks it on his bed, army surplus. He removes the clean and beautifully folded clothes and his one bath towel, arranges them in low stacks under the bed. His tea towel will drape over the edge of the dish drainer. He puts the pillowcase back on the pillow. He washes the sheets once a month, they need a machine all of their own and cost extra. Next week.

Drifting, drifting, drifting. Jackie drops on to his bed, buries his face in the fresh pillowcase. The coolness, the supple moulding of the light cotton to the contours of his nose and cheeks like a pair of hands cupping him. Applying the gentlest pressure for healing the ache that is moving from behind his eyes to the bones of his face, a heat welling up around his eyes. Bobby Wilmot, and now there is no escape, he is being drawn back and starts to have the nightmare, awake.

He is running but getting nowhere: Frank is coming. There is the knock on the door. Don't answer it, Jackie.

But he did answer and Frank said, Hey, there's something going on in the building where I work, sixth floor, you might be interested, Molloy. In fact, I know you'll like this situation, there's this guy, see, a boss, Chuck Wilmot, and his secretary, Anna Laskowski, and then of course there's the boss's wife, Marilyn, plus three kids. I run them up and down in the elevator to his office, they like to visit the old man on the job, you know, they come into the city from Levittown.

Jackie grips the sides of the pillow, clenches his teeth, bashes the pillow. Frank keeps talking, will not be silenced.

I think this guy Wilmot has a girlfriend, that's right, Molloy, no question about it, and I think the wife and the secretary know about this little hanky-panky, and you want to know what I think? I think they aren't too thrilled about it. But for you, hey, I think there might be a real good time, you need it, you're lonely again since the Mulligans left. You come around to me this week and I'll point them all out and off you go. You just fix me up, I'm a little short these days, and I'll put you on to this, you'll get your rocks off real good, Molloy. So how much? Okay, beautiful. I'll keep you posted. See you on – Wednesday? Perfect. Wednesday it is, you won't regret it. What? Oh, no, I won't breathe a word about our little secret, Molloy, Mum's the word, on Wednesday you just bring along some of the nice green stuff and we'll all be happy.

Two and a half months of tracking, following, watching. From January, dark of winter, seeds covered, hibernation, until the day. All that a jumble now like the clothes in the dryer. Inchoate memories, nothing put together, no one image connected to anything else recognisable. His mind cut and pasted, pastiche history, no coherence. Which came first? When did he know? What had he done the next day, the next moment?

Run, Jackie, run. Go to her, go to all of them.

Which instant was it when he saw so clearly and has never seen any moment with such certainty again? Suddenly he knew it would happen, and he ran to stop it, but too late, the train had left the station and was pulling out of reach. He was in the wrong place at the wrong time.

For the wrong person.

All wrong.

And now on the bed his legs are pumping. He is roaring into the pillowcase, spewing saliva, he is working the pillowcase with his lips and teeth, 14 March 1959, too late.

And then the next step in the horror: Marty, now Editor of the *Mirror,* is approaching Jackie's desk, hands in his pockets, that grin. That unmistakable grin. Holding the police report. The autopsy report. Jackie is his star, Jackie will make him first with this story, no story Jackie can't handle, he has won two awards for local reporting, the up-and-coming, the next one-and-only.

How about it, Molloy? He winks.

Answer him, Jackie. You know what he's asking. This is how he always does it, when a big story breaks and you're it, he wants the best and no nonsense, he comes to you with that grin and that wink as if you have a choice. The story he wants. The story to make the *Post* and *The Times* and the *Gazette* and his mother in Westchester squirm. To him every story he comes across is the biggest story ever, we'll fuck them down at the *Post,* Jackie, we'll see who's got the biggest dick. He uses stories to screw his competitors, stick it to them with the big dick story.

Does he know, or sense, what Frank knows about Jackie?

Is that what the wink means?

The Wilmots and the girl were supposed to be a private story, a private investigation, all wrong now, and sure enough, Jackie's worst fear, the whole town, every newspaperman, jumping at this story, and here comes Marty. Put it off as long as you can, Jackie.

How about what, Marty?

You're kidding me, right?

Get off my back, I'm working on the Dodgers story.

Fuck the Dodgers, Molloy. You're not working on that any more. You're working on this.

Police report and autopsy. Smacked on the desk.

Oh, Christ, Marty. It's not an exclusive any more, never was, it's old news. Ants crawling all over this story.

Hey, Molloy. You're not listening. What I'm telling you is I want you to be the biggest ant in the shitpile. I want you to get out there and interview these people. Because everybody knows one of them did it and *you* are going to find out who, you got me? Which one of these scumbags strangled that girl. The cops don't know, the *Post* don't know, *The Times* don't know, but *I* want to know. Understand? I want you to do the biggest story of your life. You go interview these people, haul your ass out there and go meet these creeps, the readers can write in saying who they think did it and then bingo: in the final story you'll tell them. We got papers to sell, Molloy. You understand me?

Pats Jackie on the back. Grins. Turns. On his way out he looks back and winks again.

Oh, Jackie, what cruel, cruel twist. It grabs you, tightens, you double over your desk, pretending to sleep, longing to sleep. Fate is a wrestler, clutches, releases, clutches, plays with you, lets you think each time that it has released the hold, and then grabs again and again with a vengeance. You bolt from your chair to the toilet and sit trembling, holding the sides of the cesspool as the foul accumulations pour out. Finally you stagger back to your desk, cannot sit on your soiled, burning anus, and standing, you sweep your withered palsied arm across the desk, scattering the Dodgers in all directions as silence spreads through the newsroom and your colleagues stare.

Thirty-five years ago.

Thirty-five, thirty-five, and suddenly Jackie is rising from the bed. Himself an apparition like Bobby. He is standing.

He is staring. Another door, will there ever be an end? The closet door. Now he is opening it. He shields his face with his arm as papers and boxes and stuffed shopping bags fall. He presses himself against the mountain of remnants, dusty, filthy yellowed books and papers, but they refuse to be shoved back in. His shoulder against the morass, Jackie pulls. A bag, a folder, a box. Tumbling. Crash. Contents strewn.

Somewhere in the rubble a clue? Some encoded speck of dust containing reasons for wrong, wrong, wrong on 14 March 1959?

Jackie scrapes over box lids with his fingernails, an excavation, and finally, on one large broken-down box lid he finds beneath the soot he rubs away: TRANSCRIPTS, BEGINNING MARCH 1959.

Only one story in March 1959, only one story ever, this is the clear thing, one story again and again. The fateful box is lugged, the collision of the others with the floor unheard, as all the bits and aspects of Jackie Molloy fall out.

He straddles TRANSCRIPTS, BEGINNING MARCH 1959, and hauls it to the table, opening, opening.

8

Hi. Jackie Molloy. Have I got the right time?

Uh, yuh. Chuck Wilmot. Nice to see you, nice to see you. Make yourself at home.

I'm going to write all this down, then I'll put the tape recorder on. You okay with that?

Oh, gosh, yes. Why would I mind you recording us? Good Lord, that's the least of my problems.

Fine. I'll plug it in over here. Testing, testing. Now. All set.

Look, I, uh, just one thing before we start, hopefully you don't mind if I ask *you* a question, that'll be a switch, I bet.

Go ahead.

Am I right to assume you'll be talking to the others? To my secretary, Anna Laskowski, and my wife, Marilyn?

Yes. And to the police.

The kids?

I, uh, don't believe in that.

Then. Okay. Because as I said to you on the phone I have absolutely no objection to meeting you, none whatsoever, I certainly want to help in any way I can, and golly, maybe you can even help *me*, it's just if I were the only one you planned to talk to you wouldn't get a balanced view, which I imagine journalists look for. Balance. I'm under a lot of pressure right now, the police think I did it, you know that.

So I'm not myself, not thinking straight. I probably won't make much sense.

I'm sure I'll be able to follow you.

And just so you know, I didn't do it.

Do what?

Kill her. I didn't kill her. That's what you're here to talk about, isn't it? I mean, the whole point is who did it, and it wasn't me.

Uh-huh. Okay. But first let's be sure you understand from what I said on the phone why I want to talk to all of you.

Yeah, you want to do a story on the whole situation, try to figure out what happened, or should I say *why* it happened since we all know *what* happened, and maybe shed some light on things.

That's basically it, yes.

And I'm agreeing to talk to you because I have nothing to lose. Somebody else on your paper already printed all the gory details, the affair, how she was killed, the murder scene. So there's nothing to hide. In fact, I bet you'll be able to find the real killer and prove my innocence.

As you say, I'm not interested in the gory details. But I'm also not in the whodunit business. I'm not here to figure out a way to clear your name.

You never know what you might turn up, though, do you? I'd trust a reporter to get at the facts quicker than I'd trust the police. You ought to see how they go about it.

So you'd like me to get facts.

Yes. Yes, I would. Nobody seems to believe me so I want you to put the facts on record.

And what facts would those be?

Well, I – how would *I* know?

Who else would?

Look, I don't want to be difficult, but you're the one writing the story. I mean obviously we want to cover whatever points *you* come up with, whatever occurs to *you*. Being new to the situation you probably have a fresh eye, and then maybe the relevant facts will be clearer.

Simply tell me which facts you think are relevant. That's not such a complicated instruction, is it?

Oh. Yuh. Well. As I say, I'm not the only person in all this. Hey, look, this is a very strange way of going about it, that's just my opinion, I'm sure you know your job – but how will I know which facts to mention if I don't know what you're looking for? Do you see what I'm saying? I might go on and on and then maybe in the end none of it would be important and you would have wasted your time.

For Christ sake, Mr Wilmot, just begin somewhere.

Somewhere. Okay, okay. You're the boss on this one but don't say I didn't warn you. And hey – you don't have to get touchy. The cops aren't accusing *you* of murder, are they?

No. Sorry. I – I'm tired. I didn't mean to snap at you.

Well, all right. Apology accepted. I'm trying to be co-operative.

Chuck reminds you now, doesn't he, Jackie, of the battle to to your wits' end for control. You wanted to scream at him, foul him with all his lies. You could barely stand the sight of Charles J. Wilmot III. But you had to. Already Marty wanted progress: who did it? Why'd they do it? When's the first piece coming? You took a deep breath at that moment in the first interview and told yourself to be a reporter: I am just the reporter. The observer. *Get outside.* It's safe there, you'll manage to go through these interviews untouched and then the whole story will go into a file and be lost. Jackie studied the leg of the chair, the cobweb in the corner, a coffee cup. Tangibles in the floating landscape of the nightmare tale. Pieces of the here-and-now objective world to hold like a raft.

Wherever you want to begin, whatever you think I need to know. That's what I'm interested in.

Let's see. I suppose an introduction. You know my name. Age, I'm thirty-five, thirty-six in June. Married, three kids. Wife's name's Marilyn. Childhood sweethearts. Both grew up on Long Island, I joined the Navy right out of high school, 1941, turned eighteen, and bang, Pearl Harbor that December. So I saw some action – Tobruk, Guadalcanal, uh, and finished out the war at a desk job in California. Laguna Beach to be exact. Marilyn was home with her parents. Then I was discharged in April '45 and we got married in May. Fourteen years coming up. We lived with her parents in the early days. Bobby is our oldest child, he's thirteen, then Sally, eleven, and Ritchie, nine. Not bad, two years between each kid, which is what we planned. After a while we found a nice house in Levittown, a lot of vets and their wives and kids. It's not the Ritz but it's a good place to raise a family, nice neighbours, Marilyn is really happy there, she has a lot of friends. The job I have now, well, had, with ABC Freight, I got that almost right away after the war, my Dad knew some guy in the business so I thought I'd try it. A lucky break I guess you'd say. And I inherited my secretary, Anna Laskowski, nobody could be more loyal than Anna. I probably took to shipping because of my Navy background. Look, let's get right to the point here: I'm not proud of myself for having an affair. That's what you're wondering, isn't it? Whether or not I think it was all right to take up with another woman when I've got a wife and three kids. Whether or not I'm happy about it. You're waiting to see if I'll defend my behaviour, try to come up with some feeble excuse for why I did it. Well, let me tell you something, buddy, I've known a lot of guys over the years who cheated on their wives and it's the same goddamn story over and over, I've never heard one good reason. Does that surprise you? That I won't defend myself? Of course it does, because I know what you're thinking: you're thinking, this hotshot is about to tell me it was *love*. He's going to sit there and tell me with a straight face he *loved* this girl. And then you'll laugh – I used to laugh when guys said that to me, they all say that – you'll laugh and then you'll say, sure, Wilmot, you loved her, that's what they all tell themselves.

Did you?

Huh?

Did you?

I already *told* you I didn't kill her! Why are you bringing that up again?

No, Mr Wilmot. I am asking did you *love* her. Not *kill* her.

Love her? Hey, now just hold on a minute, how did we get on to *this*?

You mentioned it.

I didn't mention it!

You said I must be thinking you were going to tell me it was love.

I mentioned what I thought *you* were thinking! And now look. I was right. You're the one with that whole question on your mind and now you're wondering if I did love her, how do I feel that she's dead. Isn't that right? Well, how do you think I feel? Somebody got murdered here – *she* got murdered – and I don't think I like your approach. You're supposed to ask the questions and I answer them. All you've got me doing now is rambling, I'm making no sense at all. My opinion is if you can't do this right, just get out and we'll forget about it.

So you want me to go now, is that it?

Yes. You've got your background. Leave. You cold-hearted bastard.

I'd like to talk with you again if I could. I know it's upsetting.

Damn right. I don't usually call people names. Come back when you don't plan to push me around.

Okay.

Look, it's nothing personal, it's just that I can't afford to lose control. There's a lot I have to figure out. I'm not as lucky as you, sitting over there. What do you care how this turns out?

I'll phone and you can tell me if you're ready.

You never flinch, do you?

This is a job, Mr Wilmot.

Not to me. You can't just walk into people's lives, dig them up, and then walk out again. What about us, the ones who don't get to leave?

Okay, that's enough.

Yeah, well, before you turn that thing off I'd like to know what your agenda is, buddy, let's get that on the record while we're at it.

I think we'll finish now, Mr Wilmot. I'm not the one being interviewed.

For Christ sake I've never seen such—

Jackie drops the transcript. No more, no more.

The swagger, the ice. Oh, yes, the cool pleasure of disavowal, the early interviews under anaesthetic. The chambers where he'd stored the accounts from his larceny, cell blocks of dry ice, ice-bound impervious cell walls, mercifully numbed transactions. If only he had been able to remain the great reporter, observer of the facts of others' lives, this is a job, Mr Wilmot.

The ones who don't get to leave.

Jackie fumbles in his kitchen drawer for the cerrated steak knife.

He howls as the blade saws through the flesh on his arms, useless impotent stumps teeming at last with warmth and colour. He stands like a post as tears, salt, and blood irrigate the carvings.

And moisten the parched, cracked linoleum beneath him, his dried up leather shoes.

9

Long Island Railroad, Penn Station to Hempstead, fifty minutes. Taxi to Levittown, eight minutes.

The Island Trees area of the development is off the Wantagh Parkway, north and south of the Hempstead Turnpike.

Levittown: a vast circuit board of curvilinear roads and 17,500 houses stamped out of inert potato fields. The rows run in to and upon each other like worms. Seen from the sky on a scorching day through wobbling air, the wriggling, squirming lines seem to tangle, untangle, and merge again as the eye strains and ultimately fails to distinguish individual parts from the sprawling devouring whole.

Jackie's car on the seven thirty-nine out of Penn Station is empty. Too early, too late, he cannot tell. He is travelling against the rush hour and as he moves out of the city, trains bound for Manhattan lurch past him, stopping, starting, stalling, delayed. Commuters packed inside stand fixed, arms clamped to their sides, propped against each other like freight for a wax museum. As if their feet are chained to the floor of the carriage, they tilt and jolt upright, tilt and jolt upright, with each punch of the train. Their glazed eyes stare through bodies, space, and time without contact. Life a thing of the past.

Jackie's forearms twinge under the sleeves of his shirt.

He has cleaned and bandaged himself, decided he won't need stitches, doesn't want doctors, and finds peace in the rhythm of his throbbing veins. The pain prods his skin like the pulse of a clock. His wounds are a timepiece, then and now, then and now, click-clack, click-clack, train rails extending from one dimension into another. A bag of transcripts rests on the floor between Jackie's legs.

At Mineola Jackie's train turns away from the North Shore. Not the path Jackie takes for his journey, his story. A fork in the road, a choice. He parts from the roll and sway of gentle hills where curvaceous roads, fingers of a long glove, drape across the landscaped contours of élite addresses. The glove reposes like the hand of a countess lying among her gems and stones: the mansions of the North Shore are jewels of space and light, assumptions not available to Jackie Molloy.

The train seems to flatten and crawl as it enters the low concrete plain surrounding Levittown. Jackie sinks into the cracked vinyl banquette, braces his knees against the seat in front of him, and rests his head. He has not slept since leaving Miguelito and unearthing the transcripts, and he is not sure he will be able to find the Wilmots' old house.

At the time, he went there so often, knew the maze of streets and greens and carports and pools so well, that he had never written down an address: the house used to leap at him from the morass. The other boxes lining the artificial roads and pathways would recede into dim light, a backdrop, and at the moment he sighted the Wilmots' from his various points of concealment, it thumped like a heart. Once he had even whispered to the house to be quiet, unable to separate his own circulation from the flow of the story.

There is one taxi at the station, the driver slumped behind the wheel, asleep. Jackie knocks on the window. The man scrambles to sit up, banging his head on the door.

Shit. Hey – what's your problem?
I want to go to Levittown.
Huh?
Levittown. Roll down your window.
This hour of the morning? You gotta be kidding.
Unlock the door.
Whereabouts exactly in Levittown? They got a few thousand houses out there, pal. You better know where you're going.
Island Trees. I'll figure out which house.
Hey, you don't look so good and I'm not driving around in circles while some nut twiddles his thumbs.
I'll know.
You better.
Jackie enters the maze. Circles, lines, shops, greens. The Alice's Teacup Ride on Coney Island, bumping, spinning, colliding with pylons of memories that push back, won't let him pass. Yes, these are the houses. Were the houses. Levitt's original Cape Cod rentals, 1947. By 1994 extensions and improvements, but still the same unmistakable square boxes on an assembly line of grass with other square boxes, each one stuck on a concrete slab. Kitchen, living room, bathroom, two bedrooms. No fencing allowed, no clotheslines. No divisions, barriers, disharmony. Togetherness.
Farmyard Lane! Turn here! This is it.
He has remembered. The house, the place, is returning to Jackie. Jackie is returning to the place.
He abandons the taxi. He runs, walks, stumbles to 143 Farmyard Lane, clutching his bundle of time gone by. He drops money behind him on the road for the cab driver, and finally, eight forty-one a.m., 14 March 1994, thirty-five years to the day, rings the bell.

10

Any trouble finding the place?

No, no trouble.

That thing's pretty heavy to lug around.

It's all right.

Is it on?

All set. Any time you're ready. Maybe start with a little background, if you don't mind.

Hey, that's me – background. You really know how to crack a joke. I'll start with the basics. I'm Marilyn Wilmot. But you know my name, don't you, or you wouldn't be here. I catch on quick. Pour you a drink?

No, thanks.

You ought to relax, I'm telling you, I read all about the pressures of post-war America, and boy, it's too much, that's our whole problem. Come on.

Steady, Jackie, steady. He is restraining his anxious hand from grabbing for a glass, gulping and gulping the golden mode of transport. But if he does that now, he may descend and never rise. And for the moment he is still convinced descent can be averted. Or at least mastered.

I'll pass.

Maybe another time? How about it?

Maybe.

So there's hope anyway. Well, what can I say, here I am just la-dee-da all by myself, boo-hoo, the poor misunderstood wife, left alone with three charming kids who are at beloved Grandma's while their mother goes nuts. You like the radio?

Umm. Yes.

I *love* the radio, I did acting in high school, we had our own little station. Being recorded gets the old juices flowing. How does this sound if I lower my voice and get all mysterious? 'Today's programme finds Marilyn Wilmot, estranged from her cheating husband, unable to get up in the morning. She has lost all purpose in life after the collapse of her whole world. The only thing she has ever known is the love of one man. And now! Now! Where will she go? What will she do? How will these poor innocent children survive without their precious Daddy, their God?' The drums roll, br-r-oo-m-m – you've got to get the sound right – 'Oh, good Christ, ladies and gentlemen! It's – could it be? – Yes! It's the OTHER WOMAN! Why, here comes that conniving little cunt herself!' Pretty good, huh?

Yes. Very. Did you kill her?

Hey. Put it this way, Mr Reporter, whoever you are: I didn't do it. But I should have. Boy! Do I wish it was me! Oh, if I ever had the guts to do *that*! Wouldn't I feel great! Something to show for myself. Look, the police have been here six times, six different cops, even some so-called lady detective, they figured I might break with a nice mother-type. Detective my ass. She was a fucking cleaning woman. That's right. You think I'm making it up? Ha! The goddamn sergeant went out of the house, stood on the stoop, and she reaches into her blouse and my eyes pop out of my head and for Christ sake she's got a microphone stuck on her boob! So she turns the thing off and says to me, look, sweetheart, they want a confession, they've got me all wired up and I got to tell you, just between ourselves, I work in the Maintenance Department down at City Hall, I don't know how I got myself into this – well, *hell,* they *paid* her, that's how, what does she think, I'm some stupid housewife? – and if I was you, she says, I'd keep my mouth shut, you did real good bumping off that bitch, the only thing you did wrong was you didn't kill your lousy husband, too. Then she tells me, deny everything, and plugs herself back in, and once again, yawn, yawn, I explain there was no way I could have done it, I didn't even know about the girl, et cetera, et cetera, I was in bed with good old Chuckie-boy when it happened, the same story over and over. You don't believe me, do you?

Why should I?

Because I'm telling the truth, that's why. She was no lady detective, she was a fucking janitor. And my story stands. I didn't do it. She was right about one thing, though, by God, I'm telling you: sweet little Chuck is the guy somebody should kill. See him over there on the mantel? Clean-cut all-American boy. The Navy had nice uniforms, don't you think so?

Yes. But I'm wondering—

Yeah? Well, you can wonder all you want on your own time, which is right now. Go on! Get out and don't come back. You've got some nerve, barging into my house, it's still my house, I'm the one in the house, Chuck is in some apartment someplace, isn't he, you'll probably have a nice little chat with him in his nice cosy little shithole where he doesn't have to think about dumb old Marilyn any more. I'm not answering questions, stick them up your ass. Who are you, anyway? Huh? You heard me, lover boy, the door's right there, you're not blind. Fucking voyeur. You think this is a peep show? Get out.

And he did.

And in a dark bar in Hempstead he drank and drank. Rode the magic carpet to oblivion where he relieved himself of the untold truths in Marilyn Wilmot's interview. Discarded them like rags, get away, get away, I will not touch that filth.

11 5

Jackie is standing on the south side of 57th Street between Madison and Park. A few feet away from the entrance to 30 East 57th Street. The offices of ABC Freight. The building where Frank works as a lift operator. 1 February 1959.

He appears to be waiting for the crosstown bus. He appears to be reading the early edition of the *Mirror*.

He is actually about to follow Chuck Wilmot. He believes that when Chuck leaves his office he will meet his lover in a bar on Third Avenue. Chuck gives Frank a light every morning when he arrives for work and every evening when he leaves, man-to-man, from books of matches all embossed: No Name, Third and 63rd.

He has been in 30 East 57th Street once before. The day Frank pointed them all out. Chuck, Anna Laskowski, Marilyn Wilmot, the three children.

Jackie had waited in the lobby from early morning, occasionally exiting from the building and returning, occasionally taking the lift to one floor or another and pretending to make an enquiry. Then re-entering the lift and riding back down to the lobby.

Frank, in uniform and cap, had nodded to Jackie the first time each of the participants appeared. Then he addressed them loudly.

Hello there, Mr Wilmot. Another busy day, right?

You're not kidding, Frank. Back to the salt mines. So how's the girlfriend? Getting any?

Oh, you bet, Mr Wilmot, I sure am.

Nine twenty: Good morning, Miss Laskowski.

Good morning, Francis.

Four fifty-five: Hi, Mrs Wilmot, how ya doing, got the whole crew today, I see.

Oh, yeah, Frank, one big circus. Hey – say hello to Frank, come on now, all together.

Chorus: Hi, Frank.

I'm training them for Radio City.

They're good, Mrs Wilmot. Got your talent. Going up to see your father, kids?

Yes.

Oldest child answers. A boy. Very correct. Twelve? No. Too tall. Thirteen or fourteen. Jacket and tie. Jackie notices. Watches. Serious boy. Ersatz man. Worried about something. He herds the other two, younger sister, even younger brother, into the lift. Puts his hands in his pockets like an executive, clears his throat. The mother lingers. He waits.

Frank hadn't mentioned that, her needing to talk. Small-talk, but still, and Frank is good at that, men or women.

The older boy shifts. Jackie can see the muscles in his jaw clench and unclench. Not the first time he has been made to wait. One eye is smaller than the other, the lens would be misshapen, he must have an astigmatism in that eye, the focus blurred. Why hasn't he been given glasses?

Hold the door, Bobby, says Mrs Wilmot. I'll be right there.

She is attractive. Brunette, hair in a bob. She and the girl match. But the girl is tidy, in a crisp pink dress with a bow at the waist, Mary Janes on her feet. The mother is askew, hair not quite in place, needing a shampoo, and the parting is out of line. The clothes are unpressed, do not quite fit, they tuck and fold at the wrong places. The body is distorted by the false contours of the clothes, as if it has been ghost-written, the true presence hidden. Except that she is underweight. That can be seen. Her navy-blue skirt, awry at the waist, is too short, not for the sake of vanity but by accident. She didn't notice, didn't care. Anyway, the skirt is plain. Dowdy. Blue sneakers, cheap, flat canvas. The white blouse under the faded camel-hair coat – the coat is the real thing, once was *it* – the blouse is tucked and not tucked.

The outfit is conservative, bland. Yes. But at the least ought to look alluring on Mrs Wilmot, even sexy, in the way its simplicity hangs on her undernourished frame. Instead she appears as tossed parts scrambled together to make the required whole. As if she has stood still while a frustrated seamstress poked and prodded and yanked. On that first day, Jackie imagined Marilyn Wilmot holding on to her hat. He nearly called out, Watch it, grab your hat, but she wore no hat. His mouth went dry and there was nothing to soothe or refresh the parchment that followed awareness.

Anna Laskowski, on the other hand, did wear a hat. Unlike Marilyn's imagined flying saucer, Anna's was a tight-fitting Tyrolean cap, a fixture, stuck in place like the rest of her, a seamless sealed package. Brown suit, brown shoes, brown handbag, no directions where to open. Her feet are fixed to tracks, she travels the straight and narrow, all signs point in one direction, Anna Laskowski never loses her way. Simple. But no: Jackie's skin is crawling. He itches. He does not believe what Anna's appearance is trying to make him believe, his skin is raising the alarm. Too bad, too bad, instead of listening, he scratches, annoyed at the interference of sensation with illusion, and turns away from Anna.

Chuck is somewhere in between Anna and Marilyn. He is clean and trim, all is in order. But he is modest. He is unsure of himself. He affects a deep voice, a command, You're not kidding, Frank, man-to-man, how's the girlfriend. Chuck is trying. Chuck is a sincere effort.

After Marilyn Wilmot and the children had gone up to six and Frank had returned, Jackie entered the lift one last time, just after five p.m. By then few people were doing business.

He stood beside Frank. The hundred-dollar bill secreted in Jackie's fist was warm and damp. He reached down as if to tie his shoe, deposited the crumpled note on the floor of the lift, and stood up. Frank twisted his foot slightly, raised the tip of his shoe, and lowered it on to the money.

Jackie walked out of the building. He did not look back at his neighbour, who was reaching for the payoff.

Jackie started across 57th Street towards Ninth Avenue. He took a deep breath. Another. Keep trying, but the feeling you long for, the feeling you had when you watched the Mulligans, that euphoria, that drug, that gossamer heroin, is not for some reason dancing through the oxygen outside 30 East 57th Street. All you seem to take in after seeing these new people is pollution. Look at you cough, ashes, what is it about them, the Wilmots and Anna Laskowski? Something present? Something absent? Something Frank didn't mention? The soot is giving Jackie a headache. He never had a headache with the Mulligans, no matter where they went, no matter where he followed them. When he first saw them, Isabelle was only eight months old, Charlie not even born, and by the time they left—

Suddenly, in the midst of his reverie, the old feeling beginning to caress him again, Jackie sees Chuck Wilmot emerge from 30 East 57th Street and look at his watch.

Forget the Mulligans, Jackie. They're gone. David got a better job, Sarah went with him. There was nothing to keep her in New York. You've got to move on.

With this instruction, the headache from the first day at

30 East 57th Street returns. Jackie closes his eyes and grinds the heels of his hands into his forehead. Then he looks up, finds Chuck Wilmot weaving his way through the crowds toward Third Avenue, and proceeds.

His skull continues to clang warning signals like a buoy.

12

Reading, reading, the story draws the little boat down the Amazon.

The tape recorder is on now, Miss Laskowski. I hope you don't mind. I want to be absolutely accurate about everything you say.

Eh-hem. Excuse me. I have a slight cold. Will that be a problem?

No. Just speak normally, there won't be any interference. In time you'll forget about the machine.

Thank you. How shall we proceed?

The police told me you have quite a clear recollection of the day the girl was murdered. In particular of Mr Wilmot's mood and actions, and of your realisation that he had been having an affair. I wonder whether you might go over all that once more.

Are you working for the police?

No.

Their involvement only confuses matters, you know. And I won't speak to you if you are spying for them. I agreed to these interviews because you assured me you would try to clear my name. All of our names.

I am interested in the story, Miss Laskowski. In trying to piece together what happened. And no doubt what I find will absolve you of any blame.

That is very generous of you, Mr Molloy. But one might ask why you are so interested in something that has nothing to do with you.

Are you asking?

Yes.

It's my job to be curious.

That is one answer. We will see.

I can assure you I am not with the police.

If you are, I will know.

Yes, I'm sure you would.

Is there a certain angle the higher-ups want you to take? In any story I am sure there are choices to be made. Emphasis, focus, that sort of thing. What to leave out. What to put in. Point of view.

You sound like a journalist yourself.

Don't make fun of me, Mr Molloy. You haven't answered my question and I feel I have a right to know what you are doing with me, and why. I am wrongly under suspicion for murder.

Of course. I'm sorry. Uh – excuse me.

You have a cough, too, I see.

Yes.

Nasty weather we're having for March, wouldn't you say, Mr Molloy?

You could say that.

Yes. I could.

As I started to explain, Miss Laskowski, you have every right to know what the interviews are about. No one is dictating to me how to get this story done or what to say. I am hoping that *you* will be the one to tell me what is important. The police tend to ignore the most significant elements of a crime in the pressure to solve it. Whereas I want to look at all aspects. Understand how they fit together.

So do I. That is the only way we will find the guilty party.

Then we are in agreement on that point.

Well. Good. I am ready to begin. Now that I believe you know where things stand. And in order to answer your question properly I will have to go over some details about office procedure which you may find tedious. However, without these details you will not be able to understand the background to this situation. It is extremely important to respect the truth and render it accurately. When so much is at stake.

Yes. We agree again.

The coffee trolley leaves Accounts Payable at ten forty-seven and reaches us by ten fifty. It used to arrive at ten twenty, but Administration did a study and found out that in the mornings productivity was below the industry average. They recommended a longer work period before the break. What the report neglected to mention was the fact that some managers were allowing their secretaries to be in place as late as nine thirty, even nine forty-five, and then, less than an hour later, would also permit the full fifteen-minute coffee break. It was quite clear what would happen with the productivity figures if this sort of thing continued. The solution was not to change the time of the break but rather to enforce normal working hours. No one, however, was willing to do so. The figures did not improve, of course, and after several emergency meetings, the report was passed to the girls in filing and never mentioned again. Now. You asked how I knew he was having an affair. I knew because I arrive at the office by eight forty-five every morning, the mandatory starting time for secretaries as spelled out in the Personnel Manual. In fact, it is not unusual for me to be at the desk by eight thirty. I am not suggesting what others should do, only trying to be accurate about my own habits. Are you following?

Oh, yes, following. That voice, Jackie. It speaks in print, too. The transposing of this sound on to paper does not soften the cold determination peering out from under delicate eyelids of innocence and co-operation. Jackie Molloy, reporter, 1959, is alert. All systems are on, lights are flashing red. He remembers being riveted by this woman's performance. This woman he had observed many times as a shadow now dancing on stage. He remembers every inch of the screen he watched during this conversation with Anna Laskowski: when he interviewed anyone Jackie used to visualise a screen on to which he saw projected his thoughts about the person sitting before him. A running silent commentary. The screen told Jackie what to ask next, what to pretend to ignore, what tone to convey.

So. From eight forty-five until nine it is my procedure to sort out the mail, get pads and pencils ready for dictation, change typewriter ribbons, and arrange packs of stationery with carbon paper between sheets. We are not permitted to open the switchboard ourselves, or to make any calls, before eight fifty-five, when the switchboard operator comes in. She is the only person authorised to set up the Daily Phone Log, and must not do so until she has connected and tested each line and found the system in good working order. However, quite often – there was no particular pattern – Mr Wilmot would arrive early, eight thirty or eight forty, and ask me to place a call for him. As he walked by my desk he would say, 'I know this is not proper procedure before nine, but just see if you can get a customer on the phone for me, nothing urgent, I had a message from him yesterday and didn't have time to return the call. His secretary will answer.' Of course, if there had been any call which had not been returned I would know about it, but nevertheless he would then place a slip of paper bearing a number on my desk. He gave the same explanation each time. But strangely enough – strangely to me, I mean – there was never a name and always a different number. I gave these pieces of paper to the police last week, and, as I said, I was surprised to find that I had kept them as I cannot imagine why I would. Only once did another secretary see me place one of these calls. She did not report me for violation of procedure because I always returned the switchboard to its original position and the operator opened and tested it each time in the normal way without realising anyone else had been there first.

How long did this go on, Miss Laskowski? I don't want to interrupt you, but it might be important.

What do you mean? Years?

Months, years, whatever.

Well, now. That I don't recall. I would have to think about that, go back over the calendar.

Hmm. And you have such a good memory for so many things.

No one is perfect, Mr Molloy.

Of course not. So perhaps you would be willing to review the calendar for me. At some point.

Certainly. I understand the need for precision. In any case it was always the same woman who answered, a very young woman. Oh, she was trying to disguise her voice, but she didn't fool me. More than once she pretended to be a man, on several occasions a foreigner. But a professional secretary learns to recognise people on the telephone in an instant. You have only a few seconds to prepare whatever attitude will be required. In particular you must determine whether the caller is someone your boss wants to speak with. If you can identify the voice quickly, you can have the proper atmosphere ready and still appear relaxed and natural, even when refusing access. In all the years I have worked for Mr Wilmot, he has taken most of the calls I put through and has had a preference for dealing with problems directly. He is known for his prompt attention to detail and his cheerful, interested demeanour. However, I noticed from the time of the affair – pardon me, I mean, looking back *now*, as I could not have known *then* what caused the change, obviously I would have had no idea – he tended to let messages pile up and quite often asked me to handle customer complaints.

I'm sorry. I'm confused. Are you saying you *do* recall when the affair began? That you did know about it?

There is no confusion, Mr Molloy. How could I possibly remember knowing something at a time when I did not know it? And I do not remember when I first noticed or realised he was having an affair and I have no idea how long he was being unfaithful to his wife.

I'm not sure I follow, are you—

Perhaps you need to pay closer attention.

Hmm. Perhaps. Well. Anyway, how did Mr Wilmot seem during the, uh, time you can't remember and didn't know?

Have you finished stifling that laugh, Mr Molloy?

Laugh?

I have already asked you not to make fun of me. I can withdraw my co-operation at any time, and I will do so if I decide that I am not being treated with respect. Then where would you be? Because I am beginning to get the impression that this story matters more to you than to me. For some reason. Which of course only you would know. I am innocent and time will prove my innocence. I wonder whether all of us can say that.

I would rather we not change the subject, Miss Laskowski. Are you prepared to go on? That is all we need to resolve at the moment. You were talking about the actual day. The day itself.

Yes. The day of the murder. That day in March. 14 March. You wanted to know exactly what happened, and I am prepared to tell you. At eight forty he asked me to place a call to her. Whom he referred to as 'him'. He was agitated.

He fumbled in his pockets for the number. I stood in the doorway of his office.

'I don't understand,' he said. 'I had it right here a moment ago.'

'What is the name of the company, Mr Wilmot?' I asked. 'Perhaps if I had the name I could find the number in the telephone directory.'

'No, no, it's here somewhere, it's got to be, I don't want you to go to any trouble.'

He started to open drawers and slam them.

'It's no trouble, Mr Wilmot,' I said.

'Here. Now. I'm sure this is it. Try to get through right away, I – I—' – he was confused, stumbling over his words, looking anxiously at his watch. 'I'm already a few minutes late,' he added.

'Who shall I ask for?' I enquired.

You were quite interested in having a name, weren't you, Miss Laskowski?

I was quite interested, Mr Molloy, in keeping the records accurate and in promoting efficiency.

Naturally.

And I do not think my present predicament calls for sarcasm, although I accept that not everyone is capable of rising above temptations of a lower order.

Thank you.

I will continue. Mr Wilmot replied, 'Never mind, it doesn't matter, the correct party will answer, just buzz me when you've got them on the line. My apologies for the rush but it is rather urgent.'

'Is there something I can do, Mr Wilmot?'

'Please, Anna,' he replied. 'Please. Just place the call.'

Suddenly he sat down at his desk. He held his head and closed his eyes. I was not accustomed to being spoken to in a dismissive manner, but although I was not pleased, I realised he was under some sort of pressure and needed my strength and understanding. As I say, it is only now I know what the pressure was and how bad it had become. I went to the switchboard, put on the earphones, dialled the number. There was no reply. I checked the slip of paper and redialled. I buzzed Mr Wilmot. He picked up immediately.

'Yes? Yes?' he said urgently.

'I'm not getting anyone at that number, Mr Wilmot.'

'That's impossible, I – wait a minute, just – Anna, try it again, please. Keep trying.'

I hope you are able to follow me, Mr Molloy. I am trying to reproduce the conversation word for word where possible, but I certainly do not want to confuse you.

Then what happened, Miss Laskowski? Please.

My, my. In a bit of a rush, are we?

No, of course not. I – perhaps you could just continue. At your own pace.

Well, he hung up abruptly. I leaned around the side of the switchboard and looked out over the rows of desks in the secretarial pool in time to watch Mr Wilmot get up and close his door. He had been in the office only ten minutes but he looked haggard. He looked like a man at the end of a long day. My professionalism requires a certain distance with which I am entirely comfortable because I understand its role and functions, but this – I – it—

Something is upsetting you?

I am not upset, I am not upset. I know you probably want me to be objective, Mr Molloy, and I am of course trying to state how things *actually* were. But this is just an opinion, and you might not be interested in opinions: it was only my *opinion* that he might be very ill. I – well, it occurred to me – I know this sounds ridiculous, you don't need to put this in your story, in fact I would prefer that you do not – it occurred to me that Mr Wilmot might be close to death.

He was, Miss Laskowski. He was very close to a girl who was, at that moment, dead.

Don't twist my words, Mr Molloy. I realise that I am probably getting way off the points you are looking for, but I would suggest that you try to remember that I am being accused of murder. That does not happen to me every day, I am not used to being tarnished with unsavoury rumours. I am simply asking whether you, in your stories, whether you – do you include feelings? You said I should mention whatever comes to me, but does that mean that whatever comes is necessarily important? Is that your approach? Because there was no reason that morning for me to worry. Mr Wilmot had been tired, even upset over the years, not often of course, he was such a steady, reliable man, but you do get to know a person when you see that person every day, all day, for so long. Do you understand what I mean? It is very important when you write about what has happened not to confuse what I am describing with, well – perhaps I am not being entirely accurate here – with, I think the word would be, intimacy. The professional obligation is always present, one does not pry or intrude. But I believe one would have, let me see, correct usage is important, I want to find the right word, yes, one would have *observations*, and one would, speaking now of myself, act accordingly. Whatever his mood, Mr Wilmot had to get the job done. There. I think that explains it.

Excuse me? Explains what, Miss Laskowski?

How he was that day. That is what we were talking about.

No. Just now you were talking about yourself. So tell me about yourself in all this. Who are *you*?

What, may I ask, has this story to do with Anna Laskowski?

Surely the answer to that is obvious. You spent a lot of time with Mr Wilmot. The police have the idea that what you do not want to call intimacy might have been a motive for you to kill his lover.

People have all kinds of ideas, don't they, Mr Molloy?

Run-of-the-mill people. Especially about secretaries and their bosses. I don't pay attention. I know what is right and what is wrong. I know the truth.

I am waiting to hear it.

Well, if you would let me return to the facts you might be able to make progress. Where was I? Oh, yes. I tried the number all day and never got any reply. Mr Wilmot left the office several times and I presumed – again, this would be an opinion only – that he was going out to make the call himself, in private. Without the confusions and interruptions of the office. I offered to stay late to finish work he had left and he was very grateful. Unfortunately I did not get the chance to complete the work, as Mrs Wilmot arrived suddenly, unannounced, at ten minutes to five. My buzzer sounded repeatedly and as I picked up to hear Bernie at the switchboard whisper, 'His old lady's on the way' – I am reporting what Bernie said, obviously these would not be *my* words – I saw Mrs Wilmot coming down the corridor.

Naturally, I said, 'Good afternoon, Mrs Wilmot.'

Suddenly Anna Laskowski is back in that room with Jackie, motioning for him to sit. Over there, Mr Molloy. The chair against the wall. I will sit in this chair facing you.

She crosses her legs and smoothes her skirt. As she used to do. Get the answers tidy. She reaches into her handbag and takes out – what is that, Jackie? – hold on a minute – it's a mirror. She is laughing at you. Holding a mirror up to your face and laughing. Jackie throws down the transcript, flings his hands in the air, something seems to fly and break, must be the mirror. Anyway, these are only words, old old words, scrolls, *her* words, *her* story, I not there, not me, a story about others. Now Marty is laughing again, too, pointing at the splintered mirror, the scattered papers, pick them up, Jackie, he orders, pick them up, forget the Dodgers,

you're not on that story any more, and Jackie kneels down to collect the scraps of lost time, he is going in and out of states and conditions, and he reads on. Almost finished this one, almost.

She said, 'Good afternoon, Anna. Is he in?'

But she did not stop to wait for my reply. She went through his door, without knocking, before I could buzz him. Excuse me, Mr Molloy. I'm sorry. Did I say something? Are you all right?

Jackie remembers telling her, and believing himself, Yes, I – I'm fine – there it is, in print – please go on, just dizzy all of a sudden. It, I suppose – it came over me for no reason.

I'll get you a glass of water. Perhaps you are overtired.

No, no, we'll just turn the machine off for a moment, I'll be all right.

You are very pale, Mr Molloy. Quite abruptly your face lost all colour, as if blood had drained away, life had left you.

Perhaps we could continue another time if you don't mind.

No, of course not. Another time would be perfect. I understand stress and strain. You should learn to pace yourself, Mr Molloy, conserve your energies. May I help you up?

No, I'm fine.

You look weak. Here. Take the water.

I said I'm fine.

Of course. Well. Goodbye until the next visit.

13

Jackie claws his way through the rush-hour crowds. As he continues his pursuit of Chuck Wilmot, 1 February 1959. Tangled Amazon growth, dark-river journey. Time then, time now, time to come.

His head is still tolling as he watches Chuck Wilmot resurface and go under, resurface and go under. Disgorged and sucked in by swells of humanity surging up and down the footpath.

Chuck turns north from 57th Street on to Third Avenue. The No Name is a two-storey wooden structure from the 1890s on the south-east corner of 63rd and Third. Its weathered oak face, three precarious steps down to the matching door with cumbersome wrought-iron latch, are out of time and place beside the steel and chrome office building to its right. The one large window holds four rows up and four across of pale green blocks of glass, conjuring up melted, forged Coke bottles. In the impenetrable depth and thickness of these square chunks is a swampy interior where light and image falter.

The low lamps on the sticky dark tables inside have red shades that pour streams of rose-water on to the cream-painted walls and patterned tin ceiling.

He has seen Chuck and the girl together only once before, when they met outside her office building. They walked to

117 East 38th Street, where the girl took out keys on the footpath and said goodbye. Chuck put his hands in his pockets like a shy teenager and nodded his farewell as the girl opened the outside door to her apartment block and walked through. A moment later he stepped off the curb and hailed a taxi by sticking out a leg. Before he got into the cab he did a quick two-step and clicked his heels together.

As the late winter sun goes down, darkness containing the No Name, a burly, friendly man comes out and turns on a rusty carriage lamp beside the door. Chuck approaches. He and this man pat each other on the arm in a silent greeting and enter the No Name together.

Is the girl waiting inside? Jackie cannot be sure and decides to lose himself in the bustle of office workers making their way past him. He will watch for the girl, ten minutes perhaps, and then enter the No Name if she does not appear.

The streetlights go on. Jackie looks across Third Avenue. What logic sets his eyes in that direction? He turns this way and that, cocking his head, straining his ears. Wistful repercussions merge, sounding from all directions and none, and then he realises he has been watching the girl emerge into nightfall from a coffee shop opposite the No Name.

The descending darkness helps Jackie. He leans against the No Name, hands in his overcoat pockets. Cold days, short days. Grains of dust, soot, and smog float in the atmosphere. The sky is invisible through this gloomy film, but the girl is clear. Brilliant. No haze or doubt. A long mauve coat, light wool. The collar is pulled up around her neck and held by her left hand which slowly massages the coldness settling on her chest. Black boots, but she is not wearing gloves.

With her right hand she holds a black leather bag. She lifts this hand, allowing the bag to slip on to her wrist so that the right can assist the left in softening the tightness of the winter air. She is fresh and alert, tallish, solid. But she feels the season. Tufts of thick russet hair spread from under the edges of a black mohair cap, brownish orange-red against black. Brownish orange-red against the pale pink-purple coat. The spectrum from dawn to dusk, beginning to end, spring to autumn to nightfall. Fire, earth, water, air. Possibilities of light. From playing on the surface to penetrating beneath and slowing, deepening, darkening.

She takes a full breath, not knowing what will be. Cannot know. When light moves from one medium to another, it changes velocity, shifts direction. How much it will change and shift, when, where, and to what end – these are measurements possible only after the transition. *A priori* calcuation cannot be made for journeys of light and darkness.

She starts across Third Avenue, also not knowing of Jackie. Of Jackie's eyes or the heat beginning to stalk him as she nears. The girl mounts the footpath in front of the No Name and surveys the area. Turns toward Jackie. He quickly steps to the curb and holds out his hand as if to hail a cab.

But not before he has noted a strange and eerie look on this girl's face. Mostly in the eyes. But the muscles around the eyes connect to the muscles around the mouth and so the cast Jackie has observed in the eyes he has also seen around the mouth. Is it a pulling? The skin pulling? Tightening? What is that? The skin stretched? How? Lips pursed. A stillness. Her face is still. A mask has been fitted.

Jackie's eyes are focused on this image, he is looking into the air, his back facing her. His eyes are clicking like an automatic camera, taking one picture after another of this strange look, and transmitting them to his brain, click-click, this angle, that angle, this feature, that feature.

She is stunning, but what is that look? Heat is gone. Jackie feels a chill. Tremulous. Yes, that's it: a coldness. He is being overtaken by ice. Blank. He shudders. Such primitive force, forces are entering his body, dangers. Impossible she should affect me this way, must be brought on by something else. Tiredness, hunger, yes, he is dizzy from hunger, he needs to eat something, anything, this following is a waste of time, ridiculous.

Jackie crosses Third Avenue and enters the coffee shop. He wonders where the girl sat and chooses a red-leather and chrome swivelling stool at the counter. He holds his head in his hands. His breathing is coming back to normal. He pictures Sarah and David Mulligan on Jones Beach. Since they left Jackie often returns to them in memory for succour, it was a soft day in May, Isabelle in her first togs. Jackie lay on a towel a few hundred yards away, a lifetime away. The beach not crowded and nothing between him and this sweet family but the balmy Atlantic puffs yanking at Charlie's little cap as he lay propped in his basket, his first trip to the ocean. Jackie turned his face sideways towards them, his eyes wandering enviously over their picnic, every item, the drinks, the sandwiches, the biscuits. Isabelle's plastic cup. And oh yes. The bottle of chilled white wine. David produced this from a small cooler. To Sarah's delight. A surprise. Then a corkscrew and two crystal glasses set on a red and white checked tea towel. David rotated the glasses carefully so they were tucked snug into the towel and the sand as he poured. Isabelle was studying her foot. It disappeared into a mound of sand and then reappeared, one toe at a time, and she counted one, two, three, four, five, under again, up again. Jackie should have known then, should have known immediately, that this was a very special occasion. Some event being marked, celebrated. Sarah edged over to David on her knees. He smiled and she put her arms around him for a long time.

Then she sat back and looked at him deeply with her hands on his bare shoulders. David had got the promotion and they were going to leave New York. You were fooling yourself, Jackie, blind. You knew he was hoping for bigger things, destined for them, you had heard them in their favourite restaurant discussing his prospects, the strategy for achieving what he wanted. You'd heard them celebrate Charlie in the same restaurant, when Sarah got pregnant. They had the same wine then, Jackie.

It is true you also heard them argue. Plenty of times. David cared too much about his work, Isabelle exhausted Sarah, Sarah wanted to go back to painting. Four years out of art college and she wanted to paint again, she couldn't figure out why loving David had made her stop. He didn't want you to paint, thinks Jackie in the coffee shop. You thought he supported you, but he didn't. And you wouldn't see it. In a conversation one Sunday on a bench in Central Park David had said, No, I never asked you to stop painting, that was your decision, and you are free to take it up any time. But you wouldn't like it if I did paint, argued Sarah. You just won't admit it, you make it sound like my problem. If I earned money doing it, then you might understand. But I'll never make money painting, I just want to *do* it. David got up from the bench and paced: Then *do* it! Who's stopping you? I don't mind if you have a hobby, but now you sound like you're not happy, that I don't make you happy, that's a different thing, that's something else and if it's true you're not happy with me you should just say it. It's not that, shouted Sarah. Then what? pleaded David. I don't know, I don't know, she cried. She got up and walked away. David grabbed the Sunday papers and wheeled Isabelle off in the opposite direction. Jackie was furious with him. Furious now, Third Avenue, present-day, recalling the scene. He followed Sarah protectively for another hour, as she sat on benches, walked, and stared into shop windows. Eventually she went home to their apartment building, and Jackie, aching to comfort her, aching for her head against his chest, watched Sarah Mulligan go through the door into her life. Jackie hangs his head like a pining dog, tears hot behind his eyes. He rocks his torso back and forth on the padded stool. Longing for the Mulligans, almost more than he can bear, and in his moment of torment he vows to stop remembering them.

Jackie slurps a bowl of sluggish soup, his appetite gone, his stomach bound and twisted. He stuffs wads of bread and butter down his throat to absorb the acid rising into his mouth. He is supposed to be working on an assignment for Marty, Marty thinks Jackie has been out interviewing two women who witnessed a bank robbery. He has their phone numbers and his reporter's notebook in his pocket, he should go now and make those calls. There is a phone right over there by the toilets. When you are tempted again to follow the wrong story, Jackie, recall the chill. Heat followed by cold: something is wrong. Call the two women and do the story you're supposed to do. Tell Frank these people you paid him for are trouble, you don't know why, but – and the funny thing is, Sarah Mulligan would want to paint that girl. What a rainbow of colour, and Jackie wants to touch it, some force is imploring him to try, while another is warning him off.

A cup of coffee and Jackie rises from his comforting perch. He thinks he has decided to phone the two women. But instead he is leaving the coffee shop and retracing the girl's path across Third Avenue.

In front of the No Name Jackie's eyes ransack the neighbourhood. Searching for what clue to what mystery?

Jackie Molloy opens the door to the No Name and descends.

14

Since his strange encounter on Third Avenue, Jackie has been to the No Name again. Many times.

But the first night is the only one to recall. A start, a finish, whatever lies between, at certain moments the gods decree that the compass will point north, south, east, or west, at a set of signs erected without warning at an unforeseen junction of time, place, and resonance. First nights lead to next days, as Jackie braves the steps downward and crosses the threshold.

He sees the bear of a man behind the heavily carved oak bar serving several customers. Others sit at tables. Chuck and the girl are nowhere in sight, nor in the rest rooms. Jackie is puzzled. He has been less than half an hour with his soup and coffee.

He gulps one Scotch and leaves.

He phones the two women on Marty's list, interviews them, and writes through the night to make the deadline.

Next day, seven a.m., no sleep, Jackie is pacing up and down the footpath across from the girl's apartment building. Chuck arrives at seven twenty, he is buzzed in, and at seven fifty they come out together and walk briskly to the corner. Jackie follows.

He boards the Third Avenue bus with them, and for two weeks afterward he is unable to see, to follow, to be in the presence of the girl from 38th and Lexington. He loses himself, and her, in work. Stories, stories, any but this one. Marty can't believe it, hours and hours into the night, Jackie does anything, covers for anybody, then sleeps on a cot in Marty's office, two hours, three hours, gets up and starts again. The only relief is an afternoon with Frank and Joanne, and afterward he tells them he has stopped following or thinking about Chuck Wilmot, his girlfriend, his wife, his family, and his secretary, they are not worth it.

That morning on the bus they were laughing, bright. Jackie didn't even need to look in their direction to know how much they liked each other. But suddenly he felt something change, even amongst the crowd he could tell they had stopped talking, and he looked towards them.

Then, then. The girl turned away from Chuck and found a small opening between the shoulders of the other passengers through which she smiled at Jackie.

With her eyes and with her mouth. He was transfixed. A supple smile, a shy droop on the left side of her lower lip. A palsy? Lips not accustomed to arranging themselves in a smile, not sure how to do a smile, more like the quiver before weeping, is she a young girl or an old woman?

Turn away, Jackie, turn away.

But he could not and did not. As if someone from behind had held his head between two hands with the conviction of a vice. Forcing him to look. Pinning his eyes to the girl's eyes.

Twist, wrestle, free yourself, Jackie, free, and after what seemed like decades he ripped his eyes away.

Too late, the intersection was upon him. He thought he knew the map, he thought he knew which turns at which junctions, wrong, wrong, wrong, and he pushed past a clutch of passengers mashed together at the back door of the bus, banged the emergency bell, stop the journey, stop the journey, God in Heaven does no one hear, until finally the driver halted the vehicle.

Jackie tumbled down to the street, gagging on the putrid excrescence as the bus sputtered away.

Don't look back, be gone. Perhaps there is still time to pull out of concurrences.

But no, his head is being turned again. He cannot avoid the sight.

Mauve coat and russet hair.

Morse Code flashing in the back window of the bus.

15

Jackie returns to the No Name.

To sit. Sit by himself and have nothing to do with any of them. Think.

Fourteen days and he has to figure out that bus ride. Get a handle, take action.

Trying to stay away, can't stay away, magnetic field. Crossroads pulling this way and that, a field of force drawing him in. He is exhausted, making mistakes, starting fights. Marty yells at him about missed deadlines, absences from the office. Jackie says he has been sick and Marty replies, We're all fucking sick, what makes you different?, and orders him to stay away until he's well, at least that way he'll know who the fuck he's got working for him.

Jackie pounds the bar with his fist. Who does this girl think she is? What right has she to do this to me? He gulps the last of his drink, oh beloved Scotch, dear dear friend and collaborator.

All right, so you figured out I was following you, well, I'm not following you any more, you think you're so clever, I told Marty to go fuck himself, I can tell you, too.

It is almost five thirty. Jackie has been at the bar since four.

Fix you another?

Jackie pushes the glass towards the bartender.

Double. No ice. Forget the ice, I told you last time and you put ice in, I don't want ice! How many times do I have to tell you.

Right.

Jackie cuddles the drink. Sweet thick honey bear, how long have I been an old man? He laughs. He looks into the mirror over the bar. He's bought an old army jacket with a collar he can pull up, glasses with plain lenses. Unshaven for a week and watered-down white paint combed through his hair, a striking grey.

You won't recognise me now. Oh, *I* can see who it is, and *I* can see *you*, but you can't see me, *I* will decide who's peek-a-boo here, who's Patty-Cake Patty-Cake, go to hell, this is Jackie Molloy, rock-a-bye baby little Jackie Molloy and when the bough breaks and when the bough breaks—

The door opens and Chuck Wilmot walks in, 5:40 p.m.

Ha! Well, here you are, you can have her, buddy, Good luck, I'm out of it.

A young man's ghost hoists his glass and drinks to the cleverer older man in the looking glass. So tell me something, you there in the reflecting pool, how long since nothing you won't do? When was that? Innocence. You know what I mean, I know you know, come on, when there was still shame. Degradation. Before the whoring.

Chuck takes a seat at the bar, two stools away, no one in between him and the old man Jackie Molloy. The bartender serves Chuck a ginger ale.

Jackie shakes his head and takes a gulp of Scotch. All he can do not to guffaw. Ginger ale! You still falling for that crap, Chuckie? You still think it's not that bad? Oh boy you won't last on ginger ale, you'll never stay alive and stay sober all at once, not for long.

Chuck holds his glass in both hands, staring with a furrowed brow into the bubbling gold liquid.

In this way, Jackie realises, Chuck is like David Mulligan: their blond good looks are not the fortune they seem. David, too, was often withdrawn and melancholy, never mind the hey-how-are-you slap-on-the-back-just-great.

Now we're making progress, Chuck, if you don't feel so good, that's more like it.

Jackie sends his glass sliding the length of the bar. The barman catches it in the culvert of his hand, refills it, and carries it back. Along with the bottle.

Jackie studies the miracle of Scotch. He doesn't hear the door open, but no matter, the girl's perfume is unmistakable. For two weeks Jackie has been in and out of department stores looking for the right one: Ma Griffe by Carven. Expensive. For an older lady, I presume, the woman behind the counter had said. Oh, no: a rainbow, madam, the gamut. You may think of brocade lampshades and matrons in dark drawing rooms, I think of Sarah Mulligan's paintbrush.

Tonight, though, Jackie smells that the saleswoman knew something about this girl. He and the Scotch decide he will not look at her. Just close his eyes and take in the essence drifting about the room on the wake of her entrance. Redolent of what? Jackie puts his head in his hands and breathes deeply.

Rich. Very rich. But this is a past glory, the perfume has begun to evaporate and darken, the light borne away on the vaporising bouquet. Leaving behind a thick, solemn, listless odour struggling to remain a fragrance. It is Ma Griffe, no doubt about that, he was sure in the department store, too, but the new bottles emanate assumptions of continuous time and place, dowagers, widows, heiresses. The Ma Griffe this girl is wearing is dehydrated. Someone made off with the light, the water, the rainbow, and bequeathed her the residue.

Jackie sways. Oh poor, poor, poor. Don't you see, Chuck?

Don't you see the poverty of it all? No, no, I take it back, better not to see, why should I be the one to deprive you of all possibility?

He turns to Chuck. Adjusts his fake glasses. The thin, youthful-looking executive sighs, runs a hand through his hair.

You're tired, of course you are, it's getting to be too much, lugging freight up Mount Everest. You can't make sense of what's happening to you, this was not what you had in mind, you're wracking your brain, you can't figure it out. Oh Christ, just as well, I can't either. But the difference between you and me, Charles J. Wilmot III, is *I don't care*. I'm on the outside. That's right. I can go when I want. *You* are hostage to illusion, not me, oh no, I have nothing to pine for, it's all yours.

Jackie throbs. The rush of blood and authority from this silent speech.

He pushes his stool aside to leave, good luck to both of you, it has nothing to do with me, and rubs himself against the side of the bar. Massages the bulge in his trousers. As he digs into his pocket for money he reaches also for his swollen penis and pumps under his jacket until he is hot and hard the way he likes for Frank and Joanne. He can walk this way for blocks, his erection pushing at his pants, the high in perfect control as he imagines along the way what he'll ask Frank and Joanne to do to each other.

He takes his hand and his money out of his pocket as the bartender approaches.

One more.

He slams down a fistful of change, the barman takes it, and Jackie pours generously from the bottle into his glass.

In the mirror he sees the girl at her table, playing with the pages of a book. Not reading at all. Thinking. A Coke is sitting in front of her, untouched. Just like your boyfriend, full of hope. You and Doris Day and Coca Cola.

Jackie swirls the Scotch in the glass, then swishes it down his throat. He puts the glass back down on the bar, still contemplating the image in the mirror.

As he does so he sees the girl push a tangled clump of hair from her face and look at the mirror behind the bar. And at Jackie Molloy.

His head jerks back as if he's been slapped. He wants to cry out. The conviction in his penis collapses. For no matter the thick caking of powder on her face, the girl has four crimson scratches running the length of her left cheek.

At the sight of these claw marks, Jackie turns with a quick jump, knocking over his glass. She stares at him, and Jackie knows she knows he has been watching her.

She probably thinks nothing of it, men must look at her all the time, she couldn't possibly recognise me from the bus, not in this outfit, in the last place she'd expect.

Jackie looks at Chuck in a fury. He hasn't stirred. Go to her, you fool! Can't you see? What does it take? Get up, get up! If you don't make a move, *I* will.

Jackie pounds the bar with his fist. The bartender retrieves the glass.

Chuck is in his own world, rubbing his temples, fingering his untouched drink.

The bartender stands in front of Jackie who is gripping the edge of the bar.

You all right?

Jackie stares at the man.

Fix you another?

Jackie nods.

Chuck hasn't raised his eyes from his ginger ale and Jackie has an urge for Chuck to acknowledge him, Jackie wants to tell him they are all in it together. But with another glance Jackie realises it is all Chuck can do at this moment to stay alive. His face is suddenly flat and inert, the eyes, nose, and mouth seem to have retracted into the skull, leaving a ghostly indentation. Something has hit Chuck full force, hit the girl, yanked them in and slammed them up against the magnetic field.

The girl has gone cold again, has that eerie, far-away, calculating look again, and she has aged, she is bitter, her skin is blotchy, desiccated, more bone than flesh. How did I overlook that? Jackie yearns for her to smile at him again, he is nearly out of his mind with worry for her, who has done this, what has happened, oh Jackie, Jackie you vowed to go the other way, why swim out to sea when the shore is so near? Why the perils of navigation in unbounded space when all you really need is one square room with Frank and Joanne? Four walls, north, south, east, and west in sight and in reach. Take the short and simple journey, Jackie, one wall to another and back to base, stay away from latitudes, from equatorial implications of unruly heat and light. The girl in the No Name is not who she appears, not who she claims to be – but who are you, Jackie Molloy, to know what is claimed or not, real or imagined? You who have never been close enough to hear words exchanged between them? In public they mumble quickly into each other's ears and withdraw, or say nothing, nothing seems plenty to them, an easy intimacy of which you know not the barest.

Jackie clutches his drink, steadies himself, and sits back down on the bar stool. He will leave in a moment, just give me a minute to get myself together and then I'm going. Chuck hasn't moved. Ease yourself up, Jackie, you'll be fine, and as he turns away from the bar he sees that the girl is now standing, oh Jackie she is now observing you, her dropped lip, uneven smudges of cheap powder clogging her pores, puffing out her eyes, infecting the gashes, a fake softness that is beginning to dry and crumble, crumbs already on the mauve coat. She picks up her book and moves away from the table toward a door at the back of the bar room.

Chuck looks at his watch, pays the bartender, and he too gets up.

Jackie is trapped. Which way to go? The girl passes through the door and closes it as Chuck leaves his place to follow her, appearance casual, appearance of actions of no consequence, and the other customers attend only to their drinks and companions. Jackie turns this way and that, confused needle on the compass, pull from all directions, where oh where?

The bartender exits to the kitchen. Jackie gets up and weaves himself in the direction of the door through which Chuck and the girl have disappeared. A few steps, wait. Hold the table, you're all right. A few more, almost there now.

He opens the door. A hallway beyond. And: a staircase. Of course. A boarding house in the old days. Rooms upstairs. Jackie has discovered their secret.

He peers back into the bar room. The bartender has not returned. He eases the door shut and mounts the stairs.

16 S

Oh, so it's you. Mr Persistence.

Any chance of talking again?

Yeah, sure. Why not. If you call this talking. I was a little under the weather last time.

Sorry the way I barged in.

It wasn't your fault.

Fault. A difficult one in this case.

Boy. You don't waste a minute, do you? Right down to business, wham bang. But there's no answer to that one, is there? Whose fault something is. If you don't say what's the 'it'. The affair? Her murder? My life?

Oh, yes. It was in this interview that Jackie remembers feeling he might not manage without a drink. He was determined to steel himself, do the job, and move on. With effort he walked past the bar in Hempstead en route to the Wilmots'. But thought at the time: maybe Marilyn will offer again. Maybe I will accept. Marty will never know. Facts outside were steadily worming their way inside. Boring holes in the barricades, weakening lines of defence. More and more frantically Jackie was searching for material to shore them up. Marty refused to allow any more delays, Jackie kept putting off each interview, each step nearer the damaged centre of the story. Maybe Marilyn will offer the drink before we get there.

You tell me.

All right then. I pick the affair.

Why?

First of all because I'm not absolutely positive who killed her. I have an idea, mind you, but only an idea and I'm sure as hell not telling you. Second of all, my life is – hey, what can I say? – my life is my life. That's it on that subject. So, yeah, when you go and ask me 'Whose fault is it?', I think of the affair. Which proves how selfish I am because the affair was my fault. So that's the first thing I think of: me, me, me. According to Chuck anyway.

How could the affair have been your fault? Chuck is the one who did it. He doesn't deny it.

I'm a lousy wife, mister. That's why it was my fault. You're obviously not married if you have to ask a question like that.

What do you mean, 'lousy'?

What anybody means, don't play dumb. Not caring. I don't care about anything. Except myself, of course. Look at the place. Not exactly Buckingham Palace.

They have maids in Buckingham Palace.

Listen to you! A sense of humour. Hey – quit being nice to me, quit trying to smooth it over. You think I'm some kind of a jerk? It's about time I faced up to my responsibilities. What else do I have to do besides clean the place and match up his socks? Not a lot to expect of a grown woman.

And the children.

The children, oh yes, well, you haven't had the pleasure of meeting my husband's three lovely children. I don't keep them clean enough either. According to Chuck. And sometimes I mix them up, forget their names.

According to Chuck.

Right you are. We ought to call this interview, 'M. according to C.'.

What about according to you?

Don't be ridiculous. There *is* no me, Mr Reporter. I don't have opinions. And if I do – here's a direct quote for you from the world of Charles James Wilmot III – if I do, they are 'uninformed because I never go out into the BIG world'. And PS, just in case you didn't notice last time: I also drink just a teeny-weeny bit too much. So all in all I'm what you might call cancelled out. I'm like that box you can check on the form to renew your licence: not applicable.

But you just said you think you know who the murderer is.

That's different, my having an opinion on who killed that little cunt. Pardon my French, turns out I *have* got a little culture in me. Chuck thinks I lack *class*, might hold back his advancement in the BIG world. Like the Rockefellers are looking him over. Sure they are. You think ABC Freight is the big world? So does Donald Duck.

I still don't understand why having an idea about this case is different.

Because it's not difficult! Isn't it obvious who would have wanted to knock off that goddamn bitch? Hear the drum roll? Br-r-oo-m-m! Surely even you, my dear Watson, have dredged up enough muck from the bottom of this cesspool to figure out the obvious.

So tell me. I'm not as smart as you.

Ho-ho, and I'm Santa Claus. Look. The cops are convinced it's me. Fine. Let them think what they want. Gives them something to do. Besides, it's my dream come true! I'm finally at the centre of my own life. The leading lady in a Broadway musical, every number a song and a dance. Big step up from radio, for Christ sake. Sorry. I'm getting carried away. As Chuckie would say – wait, hold on, I've got to whisper to get it just right, and put my hand lovingly on your shoulder – 'Honey. Keep your voice down. Okay? That's a girl.' Nice, huh? You've heard of grey? That's how my Chuck likes his people. So you're probably wondering why I miss him so much.

I hadn't noticed.

Aren't you a wiseguy. Well, I do miss him. That's the mystery of love, isn't it? The way you come back for more. When it's bad, that is. You ought to meet the gals around here. The happy ones are miserable. Can't stand the guy if he's nice to them. They envy me.

You laugh. Okay. But I'm telling you.

Telling me what?

I'm telling you if he's a bastard then you know where you stand. Narrows down your problems, less to worry about. You know what you're dealing with. Otherwise there's nothing. A nothingness. Can I offer you a drink? A little pick-me-up. Don't worry, I know what I'm doing. The trick is to stay in control.

No, thanks. Not on the job.

Aw, come on. You're too serious. Just a small one. You said maybe next time. This is next time! Life moves on! A little one. That's all I ever have. You'll be fine.

Well, I – not too strong.

There you go now, that's it. Booze concentrates the mind. You're too stiff. You ought to loosen up. Hey – why *are* you so nervous anyway? I'm the one who's supposed to be nervous. First time you ever had a drink with a killer?

Speaking of which, when are you going to tell me about the belt?

My, my. Just as the happy couple settle down for a nice afternoon.

You mean you weren't going to bring it up?

I wasn't *not* going to mention the goddamn belt. Why

would I try to avoid mentioning something everybody is talking about already? Huh? Don't underestimate us Levittown housewives.

I don't.

I mean, wouldn't I stand a better chance trying to avoid talking about something you *don't* know about? Prevent you from discovering it? Now that would be good.

Good fun, all right. What's the 'it'?

There is no 'it'. I'm just saying *suppose*. *Suppose* there was something you didn't know that I did know, then that would be the thing to hide from you. But there isn't anything.

Really?

You think I don't know what I'm hiding and what I'm telling? For Christ sake. You can do better than that.

The belt.

You want me talk about the belt, fine, I'll talk about the belt. You know how many of those things B. Altman's sells every year? How obvious can you get! You think Chuck or I would use something that would link him or me to the murder? Please. Besides, my belt is right where it belongs: gathering dust in the closet. I never wear the stupid thing. And I don't haul it out every once in a while to strangle somebody.

Why don't you wear it?

What has that got to do with anything?

Maybe we'll find out if you just tell me why you don't wear it.

Push push push. Okay. That belt is a piece of shit. Satisfied? Given to me by one Charles James Wilmot III to put with a dress he bought me for a Navy reunion one of those years, shit on shit, who the hell can remember what year, one and then another, blah, blah, blah. Freshen up that drink for you?

I—

That's a yes. Now. Isn't that better? He thought I should spruce up my image, you know. And smile more.

How was the reunion?

We didn't go. Sally got sick. Kind of just a cold at first, so I thought, but she wasn't herself, listless, glassy eyes, stiff neck, no appetite. Her temperature went up and up and my usual remedies didn't help, drinks, cool baths, hugs. I'm a sucker for hugs. See how this wine loosens the old tongue? You'll start to think I'm a softie and trap me with one of your sneaky questions. But you won't. I'll be too quick for you. And stories, yuh, I read her a lot of stories, Sal and I love a good story, my Sal, so we did all that, and there was His Majesty going on and on about how she'll be fine, we're still going to the reunion, like he could make it go away – in fact, that's a very good point, if I do say so myself: Chuck can't stand reality, just wants to make everything be the way he wants it to be, never mind the real world. People, for instance. Never mind *people*. 'We'll just get my mother in as planned,' la-dee-da. See, it was his big chance to show me off in the new dress and tell everybody he was – are you ready for this? – VICE PRESIDENT OF ABC FREIGHT! And the belt – don't worry, I didn't forget your precious belt – he wanted to show off the lovely new belt. But lo and behold, after the second housecall from the doctor, the doctor says, she's not getting better, I don't like the look of this, and boom, into the hospital with her: meningitis. And that was the end of the reunion. He wouldn't go by himself, oh no, the whole point is to show off the wife, so he stayed home with – let me see, did we have Ritchie then? Oh, anyway, it doesn't matter, he stayed home with Bobby. And somebody else. Come on, guess who?

Not after two drinks.

MOTHER!

His mother.

'I love her so much, Marilyn, she's so good to me.'

Obviously you like her.
You're pretty sharp.
How long was Sally in the hospital?
Let's see now. Oh, the poor thing was there a long time. Almost two weeks I think it was.
Scary.
Scary? *Scary*? Are you kidding? You don't know what fear is, buddy-boy. She was petrified. I was petrified. Zap. Like an electric shock running through you, your hair sticking up like a porcupine. I didn't sleep a wink. Right there in the room with her. I wasn't going anywhere, wild horses couldn't keep me away. They tried to put visiting hours on me, claimed I would disturb her, but I refused to leave, she refused to let go of me, the two of us screamed bloody murder when they tried to pry her fingers off my arm. Then finally the doctor authorised me, I AUTHORISE THIS WOMAN, and they brought in a bed. Would you leave your child alone with a bunch of strangers? All full of big ideas, you know, like, in a real deep voice now, 'Mrs Wilmot, it would help your daughter if she could relax.' Oh, really? Hey – if that's all it takes, even you and I could have been doctors.
I wouldn't have left her with them either.
Yeah, well, like hell, 'relax'. I know you wouldn't and I didn't. I told one of them to shove her rule book up her ass, this is my child. Charming little C. just ran around apologising. 'My wife's a little upset, sorry, sorry, she gets like this.' You're damn right I do.
She recovered?
Totally. I slept in the bed with her, she was shivering, delirious. Petrified. She needed to be held. During the day I rubbed her down with alcohol, brushed her hair, read stories, sang. I'm not much of a singer, but hey, Sally loves my singing.
How old is she now?

Twelve. Nice big girl. Gorgeous. She drew that picture over there. Good, isn't it?

So the kids are at his mother's.

I told you.

How did it happen?

They got a social worker in here, that's how it happened. Who cares.

They who?

Chuckie and his Mummy. Who else? The two of them have to be better than everybody, Marilyn isn't a good influence. That fucking bastard. We were *fine*! I was *managing*, for Christ sake. He took my kids! Those are my kids! They just – he – some woman came in here after school with his mother and I – they – they came in, barged their way through the door, and *took* them! She said to the social worker in that voice of hers, Look at her, look at this place, and they packed some bags and walked out, with *my* kids. Do you understand what I'm telling you? Do you hear what I'm saying? We're talking about my kids!

I – I'm sorry. How did the children react?

They cried. What the fuck do you think they did? They screamed. Listen, Mr Reporter: this is their *home*. This is *me*. I chased the two bitches into the back hall, Sally ran upstairs with Richie and hid in the closet, and Bobby, he's nice, he's the nice one, very polite, he came into the back hall while I cornered them and he asked to see their search warrant. Can you believe it? Isn't he something? That's my Bobby. We're fine, Grandma, he says, we don't want to leave, we're staying with Mom, just go and we'll be fine, I'll look after everything. The social worker tricked me, she crawled between my legs and escaped while I was holding on to Bobby, and she tried to dash upstairs to look for Sally and Richie, but I ran ahead of her and lay down across the landing with my legs up on the wall. Clumsy bitch tripped over me. Serves her right.

Now *you're* pouring the drinks I see. Mr Big Hotshot Reporter. Anyway, then she dragged them out, school books, sacks of clothes, shirts and blouses hanging out of goddamn pillowcases, the pigs didn't even have the decency to pack a bag.

You – I – how did you feel?

Feel? What are you, some kind of a sadist? Some kind of a pervert? Do you see me laughing? Do you see my kids laughing? Hey, you kids! Come on down here and give this guy a laugh! What a riot. There's nobody cracking jokes around here, buddy, they're not even up there, so it's not my problem if you can't figure out how the hell I *feel*.

That's right, have another drink, go ahead, then you might be able to put yourself in somebody else's shoes for once, and while you're at it you can shut off that goddamn machine, never mind, I'll do it for you, kick the goddamn thing on the floor, that's what I'll—

17

A clink of glasses from below. Four doors stretch from one end of a long corridor to the other. Jackie has no way of knowing which one.

A stillness. One bare bulb lighting the way.

Jackie removes his shoes and pads across the old wooden floor. No Frank and Joanne, between his legs he is now shy and withdrawn. His brain, covered in fuzz like mould, cannot fully recall how or when he got from the bar to here, where he is going or will end up, nor why his throat and the backs of his eyes ache.

Jackie puts his ear to the first door. There is no sound he can make out, no light seeping through. The second door. The third. Of course: they would be in the room furthest away from the stairs, they have no other sanctuary, and so, pressed to the fourth he hears the sound of tap water lightly splashed into a basin. A face cloth being wrung out. One set of footsteps. From the basin to a location beside the door, back to the basin, and so on. Three journeys. On each occasion there is a long pause at the site away from the basin. No words are exchanged, nothing audible extends into the outside world.

But Jackie feels the soothing touch of the face cloth against his skin and thereby sees that Chuck is ministering to the girl's injuries, warm water on her face. He should use cold, preferably ice, but facts are of no relevance, technicalities scant assistance, in the application of comfort.

Jackie hears no surprise in the secluded room: Chuck and the girl have anticipated. From Coca Cola and ginger ale, patty-cake patty-cake to a nightmare, is not for some reason a shock.

Jackie badly wants a drink. He eases himself to the wall beside the door and slips down on to the floor. Now even I do not make sound, he thinks. In the presence of injury, in the knowledge of disfigurement. Oh, for anaesthetics, but this is not the bar, Jackie. You made your decision. You took the stairs, you followed, and the consequence is echoes, the doors, the rooms, for Jackie the little boy is washed and fresh and clean, isn't he something, only six and look at him. Look at him, Al, you're the bartender, you see a lot of people, right? I mean, I could be his mother, I really could, couldn't I? Don't he look kind of like me? You'll let me be your Mommy, won't you, Jackie? Let Georgie be your Mommy?

Get up off the hard cold floor, Jackie, get a drink, get away, you'll be fine, that was another bar, another room. The presence and absence of children in the hollows of other betrayals, refractions as light and sound pass from one abyss to another. The tangled distortions of a time before now pull at layers of the present swamp, thick coats and undercoats of sewage. Light and sound contort and deform, as Jackie strains against the sucking. How about a Coke, Al, get my Jackie a Coke, there's your little drink, now show Al what's in the bag, he's got a nice truck in there, haven't you, and a Mars Bar, and dominoes. Show him.

Yes. A crinkly brown paper bag rolled over twice at the top, you gripped it in your right hand, four fingers tucked in under the folds like a latch and you were not about to show what you had in that locker, for there was also a tooth. And a nickel from the tooth fairy.

—and the most important thing, Al – come on, Jackie, open your mouth – come on – the most important thing is, can you guess, Al? Can you? Take a look in there, here, I'll hold it open for you, he's just being shy, what a surprise we had today, didn't we, and the tooth fairy gave you a whole nickel for that tooth.

Christ, you'll spoil him, a nickel for Christ sake.

Oh, no, Al, not for my Jackie, no pennies, Jackie say thank you, thank you tooth fairy.

Clasp, tiny bag, lips sealed over the errant tongue that wanders into and out of the vacant space, testing the raw spongy opening, and you the boy sucking blood, churning it with warm saliva in the dark recesses, the secret silent vault, sounds under lock and key, for sounds belong to *me*, can't take, Georgie, can't take, can't—

He don't want to talk, Georgie. Leave him be.

Hey, since when are you the mother, Al? You just look after your goddamn bar, bunch of slobs you got in here, you're lucky me and Jackie even come into this dump, isn't he, baby. Say *Mama*, Jackie, say *Mama*. Maybe if Georgie gives her honey bun a nice big smacker, that's it—

Oh oh like a probe in the cavity, the wound screams, tears slide down the little boy's cheeks, rivulets carving signs on hillocks, fire and water, burning streams brand the property, but the lips tighten, sound is a give-away, can't take back sound—

He's mine, aren't you, Jackie? You don't belong to old Al here, you belong to me.

Make Jackie feel: lay claim.

Georgie, hey, you hurt the kid.

Oh I don't hurt my Jackie, do I, do I, you tell him—

Another kiss, harder kiss, pressing the jaw, pressing with the chin on the site of the throbbing core, trying to get down and in, and now the little boy's eyelids fasten like the lips, merge to make one taut seal over deed and title.

For Christ sake, Georgie.

Hey, what's the matter with you, Jackie Molloy? Why's he closing his eyes on me like that, Al?

I thought you said you're the goddamn mother.

The other end of the bar, Hey you fuckin' whore give the kid a drink, what's Mick Molloy's son need with a fuckin' Coke, it's on me, Al, she'll smother him, you fuckin' whore, come here, kid, sit on my lap, just sip this you'll feel better, yeah, you're a nice one all right, that's it.

Get your stinking paws off him, Tommy, you're a pig.

He's drinkin' it, isn't he? He didn't say no. Sit down and shut up.

Hey, who do you think you are, wait'll Mick sees this—

You heard me you fuckin' bitch.

Al, tell him.

I don't tell him nothin', Georgie. And you better not either.

Oh, hell, gimme a Manhattan then.

See, Sugar? Nice and quiet.

Give him back to me, Tommy. Come on.

In a minute, in a minute. He likes me, don't you, kid, and besides you gotta finish your drink.

Mick told me *I'm* the kid's mother now, he didn't say you could butt in.

Slowly, slowly the retainer lifts. Softened murky eyes are out of danger, smiling behind the woozy film, floating, floating, rising above the battlefield. Now the boy can fly, he stretches his arms out, leans this way and that to steer through the blissful clouds, the raging and blazing are faint pops in the distance, the merest inconvenience. The lips part, melted butter spreads across warm pliant dough, tension kneaded out. The thick tongue cannot even manage to locate the void left by the missing tooth, this too, this pit, has lost its hazards, there are no edges. The bar room glows, aurora borealis.

Fucking pig, Tommy. Come on.

He's smiling, isn't he? Wasn't smiling with you.

For Christ sake, he's drunk, you got the kid drunk, give him back, I'm taking him to Mick.

Arms reach out, Tommy lets go. The boy slips off the bar stool, catches his foot, falls.

Uproarious din, and oh what a marvel the knee has been banged but there is no pain, no feeling, merciful release from the body, clapping hilarity boxes the ears but the ears are wearing muffs, the volume on the torments is turned down, and higher higher the little boy is carried on a stream of well-being, transcendent waters rippling through stratospheres—

Come here to your new Mama, Jackie, forget about those pigs, they're nothing – hey you jerks should laugh at yourselves you want to see something funny, you—

Rubbery limbs have a will of their own, and Tommy reaches for the patty-cake patty-cake and the boy now wants to stand up, the calf is struggling to discover his legs and what they can do. The grinning creature wobbles, tips, buckles, and finally stands, gripping the stool, swinging the coveted parcel.

Here-here! Bravo!

Come on, honey, we'll go to Daddy, Daddy wants to see you.

Oh yeah like hell, his fuckin' Daddy's in a fuckin' meeting, he don't want to see no kid back there.

And the boy's arms are now wings, his face is lifted to the sky, and he is turning, turning, gliding, skating, and the applause is getting louder, reaching him, reaching him the stubbly faces, gruff whiskers, guffaws and encouragement, a sweeping tide of pleasure, and another man reaches out.

Hey, I'll dance wit' him—

No, Eddie, no, Jesus Christ, give him back to me.

We're dancin', Georgie, never cut in on a guy dancin' wit'

his sweetheart, nobody ever teach you ettycat, hey Al, give that bitch another Manhattan, shut her up, the kid's a good little dancer, aren't you—

The dance the dance

Come on, gorgeous, what have you got in that bag, you're stickin' to that thing like it was Fort Knox, show your Uncle Eddie what you got in there.

Leave him, Eddie – hey Al where's that drink—

Somebody pays me first. You think this is a charity ball?

Aw, Al, come on, you know Mick's good for it.

And the fingers try to hold on, they have some memory of not to let go, mustn't let go, but there is no longer the resistance in these bones, flaccid against gnarled hands prising the latch. And now the bag is away, gone, never was, the Mars Bar is being enjoyed, the tooth is being passed from mouth to mouth and tried out, and the dominoes stand in a perfect line on the bar. The first is tapped, takes only the first, ashes ashes all fall down.

Chuck and the girl. Saying something – can't make out – ready to leave.

Jackie grabs his shoes, scrambles up. Go, go, must not be seen, not heard, quick, down the stairs, out, away, and in the darkness and chill on Third Avenue Jackie runs and runs, the unyielding pavement slamming his feet into submission. All the way to Grand Central Station.

Where he hobbles on to the train for Hempstead, bound for his crypt. To await Chuck's return to 143 Farmyard Lane.

And the next morning, aching swollen feet in a pan of warm water, he remembers that the shoes have been left behind.

18

Jackie rings again. 1994. Still no reply.

I want to look inside: what I did not see, might have seen. And been on time. Sit in the chair. Get a new angle. Was a clue in that room all along?

He edges his way behind two shrubs, cups his hands to his temples like blinders, and peers through the window.

Different arrangement. Marilyn had the sofa against the far wall, a chair at either end. Jackie remembers. She sat on the sofa, he in the chair to her left. The tape recorder was on the coffee table beside *Time Magazine*. Where is the coffee table? That was thirty-five years ago, Jackie. This is someone else's chance.

Jackie is on the footpath before he realises his hands are scratched and bleeding, his trouserleg ripped like his arms. He has walked into and through the shrubs. The thicket, the tangle. And felt nothing.

The small green across from 143 has been preserved. Trees, benches, more shrubs, flat winding paths. Swings and a sandbox. Brand new. Why is the park empty? No children playing?

The only alteration Jackie notices is that more shrubs have been planted. Or the old ones grown and spread. That must be it. Grown and spread. He isn't sure. The shrubs now form a hedge. It borders the near side of the green, facing 143, and the rest of the area is open. You can enter beside this natural wall, walk through the meandering footpaths to the other side, and still be on Farmyard Lane because Farmyard Lane curves around. Considered one of the nicer sections for this touch of intimacy, the soft arc leisurely cradling the green. But the only way out is the way in. To leave Farmyard Lane you must go back the way you have come. This was always the problem.

Jackie enters. Has done so time and again. Bear left at the first bench. He is now behind the hedge. As before. His heart pounds, races. Registers. Experience is knowledge, the organs memorise. Jackie has come upon his old hiding place.

At night, unseen, on all fours, he used to crawl. A space he had trained into the foliage opened for his arrival and closed behind him, containing his subterfuge, his justifications, his excitement. A tomb for the practise of deceit. Air and light would rankle. Just enough space for Jackie only.

Now he is on his hands and knees in broad daylight. No one looking, no one home, no connections.

He is back in the old spot, under cover, his chin nearly level to the ground. He pulls at the knots of clenched vines and leaves and makes his spyhole, the past guiding his fingers well: 143 is in direct view. In those days he used binoculars. Propped in a nook in the sturdy scaffolding of his natural wall. He didn't have to hold them: just set them in place, rest his chin on his hands, and his eyes met the instrument perfectly.

Go ahead, Jackie. You are here now, you have come despite. You have come because of. Take a good look, take in.

He eases closer to the spyhole, leans his head toward time past, and enters.

Chuck is being dropped off by a friend who keeps an old

car at the station. Nine forty-eight p.m. He gets out, closes the door, and the other man drives off.

Chuck walks slowly up the path to his bungalow, four and a half rooms. Two bedrooms, no garage, no large trees, no fences, row upon row, same upon same. Oh, the promise there is in each trim and tidy box, the belief in each perfect square of lawn. And yet Chuck Wilmot's head is lowered.

Jackie is overcome in the hiding place of the present. He too can hardly raise his head. He too is wrenched with bereavement. His heart is being pushed and pummelled and slapped as if the the soul were a lump of dough. He loved the old house, the house the way it was, the way he and Chuck saw it that night and many days. The reliability, the solid reputation and contentment of cedar shingles. The unbroken lines of a flawless roof fixed to a perfect square container. Regulation assembly-line windows and doors and vents and gutters fitted to each house without a centimetre's threat of variation, identical linear paths leading to each door from the unscathed pavement. Shuttle from A to B, B to A, known points of arrival and departure, finite journeys to unmistakable destinations. Jackie had never known such undefiled intactness.

The 1994 version of 143 Farmyard Lane has an aluminium siding, a white door with panels outlined in red, the lip of a second storey pouting out over the first. There is also an extension tacked on to the right side, cramping the grass. An extension whose windows do not match those of the main house. Except that all are protected with criss-crossed bars and an alarm system. Jackie rocks himself. Poor poor Chuck, he tried with all his heart to stay inside the bounds. He meant to. He meant to take the shortest route from east to west, the straightest line. Nothing but ships' holds and containers had ever occurred to him.

He is coming home from the No Name, from the girl's

clawed face. Jackie arrived first at 143 because Chuck returned to the office before he caught the train. To gather up the pages of a life that gives him strength. The life of files and timetables, memos, routing charts, budgets and procedures. He stuffs wads of these real things into his briefcase and on the ride home from Penn Station studies them ferociously.

Where oh where the answer?

Chuck pauses on the front stoop of his dream. He peers into the living room. Marilyn must be in the kitchen. He puts his briefcase down, heavy heavy heart, and straightens his tie. He rubs his forehead, picks up the case. Turns the doorknob and in.

Jackie pushes himself forward and places the binoculars in the nest of leaves and branches. Tilts the glasses slightly up, direct sighting of living room. Curtains are not drawn, for residents of Farmyard Lane like looking out on the green and playground.

Darkness completely surrounds Jackie Molloy, 143 Farmyard Lane and the playground. Except for a soft aura from the streetlights, a gentle hover affirming the peace and certainties of Levittown. Jackie blends in. This place is not attuned to intrusion. The lights are a trusting presence, merely to guide the way. Not to expose danger.

Jackie's eyes fix on the Wilmots' living room with the tenacity of a spotlight. Chuck has disappeared. There is still no sign of Marilyn. The children must be in bed.

Jackie loves the wait. Savours it. Not an empty time, oh no, not an absence: he is swollen with longing. He can imagine. And fills up with the power of his imagination to draw the story inside, aching, on the cusp of fulfilment, about to burst with the expanding heat of anticipation. A warmth that nestles him like his cave of shrubs and branches, a womb for the implantation of fantasy, rejection of reality, foreign body. Padding against the failure of outside to meet inside. Waiting undercover across from 143 is no different from waiting for Georgie and Da-da, tuck in at seven, Georgie and Da-da have to go out for just a little while, before you know it they'll be back. Don't you let anybody in our room, this room is only for Jackie, Georgie, and Da-da, go to sleep, go to sleep, and on the other side the key is turned in the lock, Jackie locked in, the lightbulb has risen and evaporated into a black sky, way up, away. Inside is left. Inside under a blanket. And by lying on his back and raising his knees he builds a tent. Lift the feet and balance on the small of his back, he can imagine down the length of the overcast tent to the end of the bed, the dropping off of the world. And by lifting and flapping the blanket with his fists, at the top, safe end, of the bed, the tent heats and expands. Let go and it deflates, drapes on to the boy in folds from foot to head, caressing him. The laying on of gossamer hands, until the weight of the covering clings to his every part. Touch. He lies thus moulded, shaped, feeling every acre of body in relation to the body of the cover, a second skin. And then the knees go up, the tent is formed, the feet rise, the hands pump, and so on so on. Hours. Contained in darkness. In comings and goings circling him in the hallways. Shivering shivering. The radiator in the meagre room is off. Longshoremen, girlfriends, crash up the stairs to more rooms. Barge into the walls, guffaw and bellow, the boy's arms encircle his quaking shoulders, the legs tuck up into the tummy, no more sleep, no more dreams. Jackie Molloy, ancient aged six, is down to the dry bones.

Dream and reality, whatever it was to whatever it is, his burrow opposite 143 Farmyard Lane, 1959, two events arrive at once, in front and behind, and Jackie snaps to attention.

Which way? Which way first?

The way of his eyes, still on the living room? Now suddenly occupied by Marilyn and Chuck who have marched in like sentries, shouting, gesturing.

Or the way of his ears? For they are alert, the ears, to footsteps on the playground. Why wasn't the intruder seen? Did he go around the side, somehow? She? Creak of chains, the person is sitting on one of the swings. Slowly back and forth, the feet tapping.

Jackie must remain steady. For the girl has been attacked. And now Chuck has returned home late, Marilyn is accusing, Chuck is defending.

No: now Chuck is accusing. Chuck and Marilyn on an indoor swing. You! You! You! You! To and fro, to and fro, while the rhythm of the feet on the concrete on the playground answers the tick-tock sway of the pendulum in the living room of 143.

Jackie shifts. Trapped. Echoes in front, echoes behind. Caught. Stop the clock, arrest the swing, be still, still in the night. Do not give up on oblivion, it is always possible, but where to grasp?

The feet on the playground have moved off the swing. The clink of chains pushed aside gives way to creaks. Shorter intervals, softer tones, then dead.

The feet. Where? Do not turn around, Jackie. No one is approaching you from behind, you are invisible. You are mute. You do not exist.

Slowly, quietly, the tap of a ball against concrete, a ghost is playing games.

Suddenly the feet are silent. The ball ceases. Back to the swing.

Chuck and Marilyn have now moved to the sofa, where they sit on opposite ends staring out of the large window right at Jackie's crypt. Jackie is trembling, gone cold. The swing has begun to moan as it is forced higher and higher.

All of a sudden shoes scrape on the concrete to slow

the descent. Hop off, run, and the ball is bounced rapidly. The shoes squeak with shifts and turns and fakes and manoeuvres. Jackie doesn't remember a basketball hoop in the park, how could he have missed it, and Chuck and Marilyn have turned to face each other. Talking earnestly. Listening, talking, explaining. Both of them. Discussing. Discussing what?

Jackie cannot concentrate, cannot fully enter or imagine, for the bouncing ball and snapping shoes have grown more urgent, their clamour insisting into Jackie's fort.

Without warning both sounds halt. Shooting a basket, thinks Jackie. Remain, remain, no one can hear your blood pounding, that above all remains private. Just continue to watch Chuck and Marilyn. For the incline of their heads, and their arms and hands meeting on the back of the sofa indicate a reconciliation. Collaboration. They understand each other.

What do they understand? If only Jackie were truly alone, the way he is best, then he would leave the shrubbery and manage to disperse himself like an apparition through the glow of the streetlights and listen underneath the Wilmots' window to their conversation. Imagining this conversation, wanting to be in on this conversation, hating to be out, this longing has a grip on Jackie. Something important – no, vital – is happening, I am sure of it. And I am missing it, can't miss, might never come back, I've got to get out of here, Chuck and Marilyn are now in ever deeper conversation, he is pacing, she is intent on saying, on listening, on nodding, on agreeing. Why in these fleeting seconds does Jackie feel such terror? They are merely making up, coming together again, but long before Jackie has seen these gestures, seen words mouthed he couldn't understand, he is about to bolt from the bushes, panic. Tick-tock tick-tock, lots of words, back and forth just like Chuck and Marilyn, Da-da and the other men in the room at the back of the bar. Loud and angry one minute, followed by hushed and intimate next, here's what we'll do, just listen, easy back and forth as oppositions reconcile.

Not only reconcile. Not make up and go their separate ways. What is it? What was it Da-da and the other men were doing? What are you talking about, Da-da? Hey! Get that kid out of here! He'll go blabbing all over the place. I told you the kid stays, he don't blab to nobody, I want him to learn, ain't that right, Jackie, you don't squeal, do you, you know what happens to squealers, and a fist punched against a boy's head sends him up the wall and down, so what I'm telling you is nobody orders Mick Molloy's son around except Mick Molloy, he's one of us, you get it, I treat him the same, he's the same or he's dead. And the tension goes.

Da-da and the other men: rival gangs. Rival thugs. The authorities count on divisions, informers. But what if the informers aren't informers? What if they're all in it together? What're Da-da and the men doing, Georgie?

Memories are darting about in the bushes and what seems an eternity, Jackie lost in eternity, is mere seconds flashing. Without warning, the basketball crashes through the roof of Jackie's hideaway. He hadn't heard the feet pounding closer and closer. The dip in the top of the shrub had become a hoop for the ball, Jackie was right, there is no net in the park. Slam dunk through the basket, the binoculars and Jackie topple.

Jackie scrambles, where to go, where to go, as he finds himself eye to eye.

A tiny pocket torch searching for a ball discovers the face of Jackie Molloy.

A gasp and the light is lowered in shock. Illuminating the boy whom Jackie saw in the lift at ABC Freight. The boy Bobby Wilmot.

Jackie hurls himself over this boy and out of the knots,

put him behind, put him behind, another child finding too much out, away, away.

But here he is again, 1994, thirty-five years to the day, and once again Jackie claws his way out of the underbrush, gasping. He stumbles back on to the footpath, back on to Farmyard Lane, and runs.

19

Landscapes, terrain, cuts and rifts, Jackie's arms throb as he pulls the cart along Ninth Avenue to Miguelito's.

There is no laundry, all was done, early this morning. Now the cart is stacked with transcripts. In order, out of order, beginnings at the end, the end at the start, and the squeaks of the little wheels turning over the footpath remind Jackie of his holding in the present moment, a thin, cold aluminium bar.

The layers of toilet tissue binding Jackie's arms are stained through with blood, dried and darkened. The bleeding has stopped. Minuscule feathers of tissue are stuck in the wounds, merged with the injuries. All safely wrapped under two sleeves, shirt and sweater.

Jackie got off the train from Hempstead at 11.04 and went first to his room. Capsule. Spinning in the vortex of the tornado that has ripped up foundations, he could not remember when he had last set foot. Yesterday? Today? Then? Now? He found his sunglasses on the floor beside a box and put them on.

He peers into the window of his launderette. Rests his forehead against the glass. The young woman who works part-time is attending to customers who are milling. She is banging the machines' portholes. Shoving clothes in, yanking them out. A radio is blaring. Where is the delicacy of Miguelito? Of course: rehearsal. He won't be back until four o'clock. Oh weary weary, Jackie closes his eyes, rubs his forehead back and forth across the cooling pane. Must sit, lie down. No. Keep walking, keep going.

He moves away from the launderette to the shop next door, shoe repair. He opens the door, the bell jangles. He tilts his head back, sucks in the leather, the polish, the sweat, all real, Tony and Marco are real. Marco comes out from the back, wiping his hands on the cloth that hangs from his belt. He stops. Stares.

Molloy? he asks.

Jackie replies: Molloy.

He turns and walks out. Pulling the cargo. And discovers the pizza parlour facing him from the other side of Ninth Avenue. He sits on a bench to watch. Bobby might come back, important to see Bobby, tell him. Tell him what? Drifting, swaying, standing up, sitting down again, still clutching at the bar and cradling the cart between his legs. The eyes roll. A flood. One stream pouring into another, which then is which? The current carries Jackie and all of a sudden he is waiting for the Second Avenue bus, April 1959.

He is going downtown from 59th Street, near the offices of ABC Freight, to 34th. Midtown Tunnel.

He could walk the twenty-five blocks. He used to walk a lot, when his body was sturdy, reliable. Only a few months ago. Not much to ask, for a little time back. He's put on weight, a lot of excess, and these days he lugs himself around like the bulky tape recorder he is hauling.

He is not following Anna any more, he is on his way to interview her again. For the series he knows he will never write. How long ago was 14 March? Three weeks, four weeks, Jackie has lost track, can't keep time, space, connections, where they belong. His mind and his heart. Churn, tangle, clog, can't come clear, nothing will remain in place. Except the girl. The girl is still. While everyone else moves around her. Eerie dance, mime, a narrative of gestures by veiled floating ballerinas. Jackie cannot hold them, cannot hold himself, all slip away, elude, disappear, like cloud formations.

He'd been calm the first interview with Anna. With all of them. He gave nothing away. But this time. This time he isn't so sure. He is shaky, he has trouble sleeping, he drinks himself to sleep and then wakes up on balmy nights shuddering, can't get warm, layers and layers, he is still shivering, demons are beginning to enter him, rock the scaffolding, he may have to tell Anna all he knows. May have to make Anna admit what she knows, face her with all the lies, hers, his, theirs, get all the pieces out on the table, fit them together. Maybe they can help each other. Help? With what? All in it up to their necks. The girl's neck.

There is a queue for the bus. Not really a queue but rather a crowd. Delays due to roadworks uptown, therefore fewer buses, longer wait.

The bus is in sight. A woman standing near Jackie stumbles. Nudged by someone behind her. As she is propelled gently against his arm, his shoulder, the touch of her, a flower brushing him and then away, reminds Jackie of his body. A sprinkling of warmth tingles his skin, a sensation of nerves severed but still quivering. Jackie remembers Carmen MacRae at the Blue Note in Harlem. He took a girl who worked at the paper. That night his body was a temple holding treasures, light coursed through his veins, electricity popped on his skin. Every pore exuded sparks, his body in an uproar of sensation as the music entered him, played with him, lifted him. The audience was on its feet in a molecular furore, and afterward Jackie was spent, channels of response drained. But not empty, no: full. Tranquillity from the laying bare, the opening of dams. The rush cleansing and purifying.

This is a memory. And on the bench on Ninth Avenue in 1994, a dream of a memory. The tremor set off by a stranger in a bus queue is a relic, then and now. Another time and possibility. In that time, before the girl, the story, and Bobby Wilmot, he would have strode the distance from 59th to 34th Street. Would have been charged with energy, in command of each spot on the path where his foot met concrete. His body used to know the way, used to tell Jackie what he was up to, register significance, pick up direction like a weather vane. All calls come through the body, the body reports truth unedited. But Jackie no longer has access to the signals. He lives in poverty.

Despairing – for he feels despair – Jackie tries to resurrect the impact, pushing nearer his fellow passengers, closer, as they crush together to board the bus. Perhaps more touch will help. But he feels nothing. His turn now to climb on to the bus, he nearly collapses. A carcass. Insides eaten away. Fetid air in a cage of bones. He has no sense of time passing, or of will, but suddenly sees himself arise and alight at the correct stop and board the bus for 141st Street in Astoria. Where he then takes the E train four stops to Anna's, 179th and Queens Boulevard. He walks past derelict warehouses, printing plants, abandoned cars. Factories and tenements. Rusty fences and dead gardens.

Anna lives with her parents in a ten-storey apartment block made of lightly-coloured fake brick. Window frames painted white, cardboard walls painted white. 179th Street extends from Queens Boulevard on its north end to Astoria Gardens Avenue on the south. Poles, Czechs, Greeks, Russians.

The street is clean and tidy, a small manicured shurb in front of each apartment building. Strips of grass lining the footpath on both sides are closely trimmed. Hard work. Morality. No mistakes. Betrayal of the old country is redeemed. Jackie's size and weight, his shirt hanging, are an affront to the order and management of Anna's neighbourhood. Jackie has let himself go, these people do not let themselves go. His sense of his own shabbiness festers as he shuffles along the street to Anna's building, watching for those he is sure are watching him.

He pulls his jacket around his paunch. His body has ceased signalling when to eat and when to stop, the relays are shut down. He doesn't feel hungry, he doesn't feel full, and here he is now, this is the result. His grossness, his punishment, his shame.

He decides to return to Manhattan. He will sit in his room. He will quit his job. He will stop the story. He turns away from the direction of Anna's and starts home.

Until he passes an alleyway separating a pair of large apartment complexes. At the end of the alley two men are arguing. Russian, Greek, Jackie has no idea and anyway does not need to make out the words, for he hears the instincts.

Jackie steps off to the side, puts his tape recorder down, and spies.

There is something here he must see, no idea what, but cannot take himself away and knows he must remain because his body has come alive. Signalling, flashing, jumping. Pain and torture, pleasure and release. Lightness spreads over Jackie Molloy, a fresh, cool sheet in summer. When he is spying, he feels himself to be the size of a bird, tucked away in tiny hollows. Invisible. Safe.

One of the men punches the other in the face. Jackie has heard this sound before, the docks: a broken nose. Gushing. This man roars. Kicks his assailant. Kicks again. A new one to Jackie, it is not karate, exactly, nor football, but somehow the leg and the foot swing and chop with the force of a steel bar, and the recipient buckles. There is no more talk.

Jackie descends into the eerie stillness, a pool of dark silences. The only sound is the snapping and scraping of shoe leather on pavement. Arms and hands dancing, the two men circle. One lashes out, yanks the other by the hair, and hops his head off the side of the building. Boxes his left ear. Jabs, grinds. Then his eyes. Pokes. Digs. The man struggles. Suddenly he seizes the other's neck and presses, presses and gouges the arteries, the victim gags, coughs. Then he is kicking. Kicking the strangler away, punching him, pulling him down, kicking him to the concrete. His ribs. Stomping his chest. Holding his head and bouncing it on the pavement. Finally kneeling beside him. Studying.

Then, with a swiftness that makes Jackie gasp, this bloodied man has suddenly rocketed up and snatched his tormentor's neck into his hands. The stranglers change places, merge, Jackie cannot tell them apart, who went first, who is responsible, and the poor neck is struggling for its life, it is being compressed with both hands placed anteriorly and the thumbs pressing on the larynx anteroposteriorly, obstructing venous return into the heart and crushing the larynx against the cervical spine. So simple, only hands and fingers, approximately six seconds.

The killer stands up. Wipes his mouth. Kicks again. Turns to leave the alley.

Jackie grabs his tape recorder. His body splitting apart. Dishes rattling on the shelves, lights swaying and toppling, walls crashing. He runs to Anna's building. Blood roars and pounds, carotids under pressure, jugulars swelling, the head and neck about to explode.

He reaches her lobby, then suddenly lurches away. Throws his screaming lungs past the tailored shrubs, the perfect gardens, this story, this story, get home, get away. Compose, restore, home, home and sleep.

20

Jackie's head is resting against the back of the bench. His eyes are open but still behind dark glasses, looking into space. Still confusing one sighting, time and place, with another.

Hey. Look who's here. My Molloy.

Jackie does not notice Miguelito cross Ninth Avenue and come to sit beside him. Miguelito removes his knapsack and settles himself, his voice as far from time present as the quiet shifting of the bench.

You asleep, Molloy? Huh? It's almost one o'clock.

Almost, almost, Jackie is yearning to descend into an eternity of darkness, he can feel his body's transformation from matter to ephemera. Oh Miguelito, leave dying light alone, let it go. No more sound. The sounds I did not hear, the sounds I heard too late, do not remind me, for if I hear you now I will recall my deafness then, my shame, that I wandered past sixty years out of earshot, let me go Miguelito, do not bring me back.

But instead the young man holds Jackie's arm, squeezes gently.

Molloy?

Jackie howls. Twists forward on the bench and bangs his face again and again on the metal handle of his cart, pain is the only feeling, he cannot be approached without it. Miguelito has touched the gash.

The young man rises slowly, his hand now on Jackie's shoulder, steadying. He places his knapsack carefully on top of the papers in the cart and in silence lifts Jackie's head and encourages him up.

Jackie's arms twinge at his sides as Miguelito pulls him like the cart along the footpath the short journey to the launderette.

Three people remain, seated and reading magazines. Miguelito nods to the girl, the assistant, she is to leave now, and then tells the customers he will finish their laundry, fold and pack it at no extra charge. They depart.

Jackie is slumped in a chair. Miguelito closes the door to his shop, pulls the shade, and goes into a room at the back. He returns with a box containing small vials of oils and essences.

He pulls up another chair and faces Jackie, the box on the floor beside.

We got to take off your sweater, Molloy. Hold you arms up slow.

A force beyond. Jackie lifts his arms above his lap where they levitate. Arms that are not arms, his that are not his.

A little higher, Molloy. I got to see what you done.

Higher, higher, a prayer for alms, the head bowed, the hands raised and fingers spread. Pleading, grasping, and now Miguelito is standing over Jackie. He has carefully pulled up the bottom of the sweater and is jockeying the garment over the back of Jackie's lowered head and the thinning wool is now bunched under his chin.

You take your arms down when I say, Molloy, very very slow.

Miguelito pulls and gathers tufts of the left sleeve down toward Jackie's shoulder. He stretches an opening.

Bring you arms down now, Molloy, bend the elbows.

Again with the right and again Jackie yields to a higher, distant intervention, his own will no longer attached to a centre, not even a perimeter. There is no core, there is no boundary. His arms prickle as if spidery legs were scurrying up and down the wounds and pin-like teeth nibbling, but the pain is severed from the person Jackie Molloy to whom Miguelito refers. Miguelito seems to believe someone is here with him, and to Jackie this notion is a marvel, he cannot feel what or who it is Miguelito believes to be present. Look at him, Jackie, he is sitting again, in front of you. He exists, you exist. Both of you are here and now.

But to Jackie these are words, and what are words, though in the past he was able to recall, if he concentrated on nothing else, moments passed in the vicinity of himself. He would even have used words.

The sweater is now off and lying on the floor. Miguelito has brought Jackie's arms down. They are resting without Jackie's knowledge on his thighs. Miguelito starts to unbutton the shirtsleeves.

If that hurts you, Molloy, tell me and I stop. You had enough already.

Enough?

Too little, too much, nothing, everything. There are no limits for the moving and breathing walking talking dead, they get it all, opportunists from the nether world find no more ready host than still-warm entrails in the land of the living.

Miguelito begins a slow, methodical rolling back of the right sleeve. The shirt is loose on Jackie, the release of the sleeve and the folding of successive layers will not bind or put pressure. Miguelito's fingers work as if they were coaxing a harp, he does not force or command. Occasionally he moves the arm by placing his hand over Jackie's, and without seeming to grasp or lift, he somehow repositions the appendage and salvation advances through Jackie like the first Scotch of the day, 1959, waves and waves of the music of the harp in an undulation that draws apprehension out through Jackie's limbs. One tributary of Scotch always began in his biceps, massaging and carrying the forearm and wrists. Another flowed across his chest, along his torso, between his legs in an inkling of sex and down his thighs, calves, and feet. Existence of a body.

But in 1994 there is no Scotch. What has Miguelito done to the stabbing biting incisions?

By now the young man has revealed Jackie's bandages. Thicknesses of toilet paper wrapped around each forearm and held with clear tape and brown twine. Miguelito fingers. Stares. Lifts the edge. Softly, softly, about to uncover.

I got to take these off you, Molloy.

Jackie raises his head. Rheumy eyes, he contemplates the disgrace. The only living soul in his time present has called at the slum and is about to open the door.

You understand, Molloy? I worried, I got to see what you did.

Dust to dust, done is done, thou art to returnest. He no longer has opinions.

Miguelito reaches down, takes a dainty pair of scissors from his box. He goes from one arm to the other, cutting the twine, studying. He wraps the two lenghts of string deftly around a finger, pulls them off like a ring, and tucks the tight skein into his box. At the same time he brings up a vial and unscrews the top. Lavender essence.

Lift you head, Molloy. That's it. Now breathe. Breathe. Like you never breathe before.

Oh sweet profusion, blossoming replenished lungs, when last, when ever, the abundance of gardens? What is taken in takes root, and only now, 1994, aged sixty, now as the essence expands and flowers in Jackie's lungs, does the corruption begin to dislodge. Jackie coughs and gags, Miguelito snips at the foul tissue and tape. Mouth ripped open, a dirge rumbles from Jackie's underground wells, oh Jackie Jackie the tissue is stuck with dried blood to the crude and jagged cuts on the tops of your forearms, and with the peeling away of layers down down to the mutilations, the wounds open again and begin to weep.

I sorry, Molloy, I really sorry.

Miguelito lays one hand on Jackie's hands, back and forth, touch touch, reaching with the other into the box for a second vial and a soft cloth.

First I clean, you got no infection yet, but I got to see do you need stitches. Not now, we give these cuts fresh air for a long time. Wounds got to breathe to heal, Molloy. What I put on you now is bergamot, for antiseptic, for relaxing. For you sad spirit. It will sting but you not going to faint, you not going to cry out, you just going to breathe. You hear me, Molloy? Let it happen, you listen to me and not to this pain.

Miguelito dabs the wounds, wipes away the blood, clears the torn skin of threads of tissue. Jackie feels the bracing rush of cool warm. Then tea tree and finally swabs of lavender. The exposed wounds sparkle.

Miguelito guides Jackie up on to the table, on his back, his head softly on fresh laundry.

Close you eyes, Jackie, you not in that place now.

Now: a fleeting moment to hold and savour, someone has said your name.

A candle beneath a blend of lavender, geranium, and rosewood. Miguelito settles himself in a chair beside Jackie Molloy.

21

The little dinghy rises and falls with the swells of the Amazon current. Borne further and deeper down-river, downward, to the point of no turning back, where tentacles gather in darkness.

Jackie's thoughts meander in and out of the underbrush until they pick up the trail. The last place he slept, beloved unconsciousness. The bench, before Miguelito arrived.

Yes: Go back to Chuck. That's what he did at the time. He couldn't figure him out. That might be a clue – how could Chuck be uninfected? Anna, on the other hand—

Never mind. No need to meet Anna again, Anna can't be important. All she did was cover up Chuck's affair. The feeling she leaves on your skin has nothing to do with this story, she's probably just like that, cold and hard. Surely her personality is not defined solely by the few brief moments of this story. Chuck is the one to watch. He cannot be as innocent as he looks. Just guide him slowly, he'll tie himself in knots. Stay cool. This story is over for you, Jackie. *They're* the ones with the feelings. The consequences. It's their lives at stake. Chuck will give himself away. For Christ sake, he probably did it, it's just so obvious you don't want to believe it. Anyway, you don't care. Begin gently. Maintain the distance.

You look like you want to start, Mr Wilmot. Or should I ask a question?

Uh, no, I'll, uh, begin. I've got, well, got, just a couple of points I wanted to get back to from our earlier meeting.

Miguelito and the launderette swirl into past tense.

You think I overlooked something?

Oh, no, items we may have passed over too quickly. I've made a kind of list so we won't get off the track. Here's a copy for you. Now. What I'd like to do is begin – actually, let's begin with point three, I don't know why I didn't put this first, I meant to – I thought I had. Just put an arrow showing that point three becomes point one, it's the point we ended on and you seemed to think it was quite important, and perhaps I didn't make myself completely clear. So we'll start with that. Right. Point three, now point one: issue of love. What we have to pin down here is that no, I did not love her. I would not be so dishonest as to try and glorify fooling around, cheating on Marilyn, by claiming I loved this girl. Right. Anything you want to add there?

No. I don't think so. You cover it all quite clearly.

Okay, fine. Point two, which was originally point one: Marilyn. I told you how I met her, where we lived, etc., but I forgot to say how much I love her. How happy I am with our life together. Naturally I'm not ashamed to admit this, I was just a little nervous meeting you for the first time, so I left out the part about M. by mistake.

I'm sure it isn't easy, talking about all this.

Thanks, I, uh, appreciate the thought. I figured you wouldn't mind if I have to repeat myself here and there, go back to things. I just wanted to be absolutely sure you were clear on this point, because I for one hope that this separation is a temporary one. You know, that M. and I will get back together as soon as the case is over and they find the murderer. The police keep implying that Marilyn and I are finished, and I really resent that, I mean, who are they to talk about my marriage? I never heard of it being part of a cop's job to pass judgement on the suspect's marriage.

They're trying to break you. Make you confess. They figure you're lying and that with so much to keep straight if they just push hard enough eventually you'll reveal yourself. And who knows? Maybe you will.

Reveal what I don't know, now there's a good one. But yes, it is a lot to keep straight. A lot has happened. And I'm doing pretty well, if I do say so myself. They haven't broken me yet, have they? In fact, and I hope this isn't boasting, I'm fairly pleased with how well I'm holding up. It's funny – here I am living in a basement flat and it makes me sort of feel like I'm in the Navy again. You know – tight quarters, lousy food. I suppose the difference is there's nobody giving me orders. I've got the place all to myself. God, in the Navy you would have killed for this privacy, to have everybody off your back, to get away from it all.

Killed for it? Is that what you just said?

Hey, I'm just talking, letting my hair down. Whose side are you on?

You're the obvious suspect, Mr Wilmot. The deception was too much. You were worn out. You had to end it somehow. Why don't you just admit you killed her and get it over with?

Because I didn't do it! And you and nobody else can prove it. You're twisting my words. What I said about privacy, that's only a way of saying something.

The question is what.

You think if I killed her I'd be stupid enough to hand you my motive on a silver platter?

You might. If you didn't know you were doing it.

Listen, I'm aware of every word I'm saying to you. For Christ sake, I still have control over my own mind, let's hope I haven't lost *that*. And anyway. I don't need to get away from anyone or anything. Nothing is bothering me because I know I am telling the truth. Listen, I can tell you, it's a big relief to admit what I did, to have it out in the open. It's not easy living a lie, I don't recommend it. I'm very relieved. Very.

I can imagine.

You know something? You're a lot nicer when you're sympathetic. But I'm okay regardless because I think I've got you figured out. You're not so bad.

What have you figured out?

The way you look for gaps in what I say. You try to trip me up. Don't think I haven't noticed. So I'm not going to leave any gaps. Ha! So now what are you going to do, wise guy?

We'll see.

Your problem is you ought to relax. You're too nervous. And you don't like it when the tables are turned, do you? Never mind. I'm not watching you all that carefully, I'm not a reporter like you.

Speaking of which I wonder if you could help me out with something I don't understand. On your list.

You're asking *me* to help *you*? Wow.

The final point.

Let's see. Hmm. Yeah. We got off the list. Okay. Right. Final point, point three. Gosh. I'm not sure myself what I meant. Isn't that funny. I remember writing that down, but now all of a sudden I can't remember what I was thinking of, what I was trying to say. 'Sequence of events/time factor/all.'

Are you talking about the day of the murder?

Maybe. Maybe something to do with the schedule that day. 'Sequence of events/time factor/all.' Probably. But what exactly? That's the thing.

Hey, for two talkative guys we're prety quiet all of a sudden.

Are you afraid of silence, Mr Wilmot?

No, Christ no! Silence doesn't bother me.

The girl is silent now. Isn't she.

Wait! I've got it! What I'm trying to say here is about the *proof* that none of us could be guilty. Now I remember. I've tried to explain this to the police, this is a very important point. The proof is in the sequence of events and the timing for all three of us. If she was killed between three and six a.m., right, then that eliminates me and Marilyn. We were at home in bed.

That's not proof.

True, true, nobody but ourselves can verify it, that's what the police keep saying, 'Anybody see you in your nighties, bub?' You know how they are, very disrespectful, but I don't care, obviously the time of the murder lets us off the hook. For God's sake, Mr Molloy, we're not going to sneak out in the middle of the night and leave three kids alone in the house. The neighbours say they didn't hear anything, so obviously Marilyn and I – or Marilyn *or* I – weren't tiptoeing around outside, and anyway, someone would have heard the car start. She says I didn't do it, I say she didn't. As far as I'm concerned that takes care of us, the rest of you can think what you want, waste your time. Next is Anna, which is the part that really upsets me, to think they would suspect Anna, of all people. You've met her, I mean, what a ridiculous idea. Is that woman a murderer? Come on.

I don't know.

Oh, I see: *you don't know*. Aren't we being cagey. She didn't do it, Mr Molloy. I've known her for years. Answer me this for starters: how the hell is this woman going to get from Astoria to Manhattan in the middle of the night when there aren't any buses or subways running? Huh? She doesn't drive, her parents don't drive, her parents can't even go out of the house, and she has no friends who drive. No friends of any kind! You know what the cops do when

I go over this? They shrug their little epaulettes and say, 'Anything's possible, bub.'

Isn't it?

No! Not in the world most of us care to live in it's not. The *real* world. For most of us there's a certain amount of sense and logic out there, most of us don't haul ourselves out of bed in the middle of the night to kill somebody, especially not a fifty-one-year-old spinster secretary, or her boss, *or* the boss's wife, all of whom live by the rules of usual day-to-day existence. The rest is pure fantasy. The police are under pressure to solve the case, that's all. You know how many people in Manhattan could have committed this crime?

But you're the one who had the affair with her. Not everyone in Manhattan. So that puts you at the centre of it.

Yes, I did have an affair, yes! And I am aware that such behaviour is not one of the normal everyday rules I'm talking about, how many times do you want me to admit it! I'm talking about *basically*. The kind of people we are *basically*. The kind who wouldn't hurt another person, who respect our fellow mankind. That's what counts, and you won't find a shred of evidence or proof or whatever you want to call it of *murder* done by any of us.

What puzzles me is how somebody like you who follows the rules all the time suddenly ends up breaking them.

Oh, I get it. Another one of those gaps you like to find, a little chink in the armour you'd probably call it. But what I'm telling you is there *is* no armour, I've got nothing to hide, I'm being honest with you.

Quiet again, eh? Part of the reporter's technique I suppose. What you're saying is, if I'm this straight, decent, reasonable guy – which I am, thank God I still have my integrity – if that's the case, which it is, then how did I end up having an affair with some girl who could practically be my daughter, well, not quite, but anyway, look, the point is to figure out who murdered her. Maybe you don't appreciate it, but my neck is on the line here. Never mind that my wife has kicked me out of the house, my boss has kicked me out of the office, my marriage and my career are dead in the water more or less for the moment, and the police are trying to haul me over the coals for murder. Great. Just great. So I'm not sure we have time for a psychology class. Who knows why anybody does anything? I really think we have to keep our eye on the ball here, I mean, I was even hoping maybe you had some ideas about the killer, who the killer is, and then we could put the police on the right track. Maybe you and I could even solve this thing.

Do you think it was a mistake?

The police accusing me?

No. The affair. Was the affair a mistake?

There you go again, back to the affair. Boy, you just can't get it off your mind, can you. And the answer is pretty obvious. Of course it was a mistake. Look what's happened! You want to pour salt in the wound?

But isn't the only problem that you got caught? I wonder if it was a mistake before you got caught.

Oh, *come on*! What kind of values have you got? Christ. You're unbelievable. It was *wrong*. Wrong from beginning to end. She was *murdered*.

So you're saying that the murder was your fault because you had the affair.

No! I am *not* saying the murder was my fault. Because *I didn't do it*. There is absolutely no connection between her murder and our affair. None.

You sound as if there is.

You are making the connection, not me. I told you: I know what I am saying, I know my own mind. You're the one suggesting that maybe if we hadn't had the affair she would still be alive, that maybe the affair explains the murder.

What other explanation could there be, Mr Wilmot?

Lots of other explanations, lots of them! Why, I – I can think of at least a dozen just sitting here right now! You're twisting things and I don't appreciate it. Why do *you* think there's a connection? You seem to care a lot about it. How about applying a little psychology to yourself, figuring out why you're asking so many questions that are off the point. And being nasty about it, too.

Speaking of explanations, how do you account for the belt?

Oh. Now you're really getting warmed up. The belt. I was wondering when you'd get around to that, took you long enough. You think that shows a connection, the fact that Marilyn has a belt like the one used to strangle the girl? They didn't know each other, Mr Molloy, they had never met, I tried to protect Marilyn. Besides: you know how many of those belts are sold at B Altman's every year? How obvious can you get. You actually think Marilyn or I would use something that might link the murder to one of us? You've got to do better than that. And I'm sure you already know the police found Marilyn's belt right where it belongs, right in her closet. Gathering dust. She doesn't even wear the damn thing.

Why not?

How should I know? Maybe she's got too many belts, how many belts can you wear at the same time?

By the way, I meant to ask you before, how long—

Jesus Christ, are you *sick*? Ask the cops. I didn't measure the goddamn belt.

Not the belt, Mr Wilmot. The affair. The relationship. You seem to want to talk about the murder weapon.

I do not! You tricked me! Ask me a straight question instead of getting me off the track.

So how long were you involved with her?

Okay. Let me just settle down here. Now. Let me see.

Well, not very long, I suppose, as these things go, I don't know, I mean, who's to say what's long and what's short? Hey – I already gave all this to the police, it's just a matter of factual information. I thought you were interested in the real story.

I am. You sound as if you think I'm accusing you of something.

Okay, okay, I'm sorry. I'm just a little touchy with all these questions, you know, the police are out here almost every day with some new theory, the one that's in charge, sometimes I see him walking up and down in front of my building with binoculars. Looking for some new way to prove I did it. I – I'm worn out. They're probably putting Anna and Marilyn through the same thing.

So how long were you having a relationship with this girl?

You call it a relationship, that's your word.

How long?

All right: four years. Almost four years. We met, let's see, end of June, and this is – what month is it? Christ, I can't even remember the month, March, April, so yeah, almost four years. Don't tell me you haven't read the papers. It's in all the goddamn papers.

I don't read the papers. I don't trust them. I'd rather hear it from you.

Boy, they wouldn't exactly want to hire you to do PR. You don't trust the papers but I'm supposed to trust you even though you work for them. Great. Well, I haven't got much choice, have I? I'm out here on my own.

What was it about her?

What was what?

Her.

You mean like her characteristics?

Her.

Right. Well. She worked for one of our big customers,

International Hauliers, she was a junior secretary at the time. Just starting out.

There you go again: silence. You want me to say more?

I'll take that as a yes. She was nineteen. Nineteen at the time. Her boss and I had dealings. Meetings. That was all.

What did you like about her?

I – oh. Well, now. Lots of things. You want me to list them?

Is that supposed to be funny?

What's funny about it? I thought it might be easier for you if I listed her traits one by one. And if that's not enough for you, maybe then we could list all the reasons you're so interested. How about that for a change? Because that's what *I'm* beginning to wonder about.

You dismiss the girl so easily after four years.

I do not! The thing about her is—

Was.

Right, was, she had a certain way. That's all. I don't know how to describe it. Always a smile. Always interested. She was going to college, very bright. Used to talk back to her boss, to anybody. Had her own mind. You could see she was going places.

She had a future.

I – well – that's the tragedy in a case like this, isn't it? Of a thing, uh, like this. What the person might have become. You know. It's one of those situations where I – you never know what's going to happen, do you? This one sure caught me by surprise.

What did?

The murder. What else?

I thought you meant her. Not what you planned.

Oh, yeah. Boy. You can bet I never expected that day I went over with the contracts – the last thing I ever thought of was meeting somebody like that! For Christ sake, she was *nineteen*. Who knows. But look, I hope you understand, this type of thing is not *me*. I never did *anything* before, I swear it. Not even in the Navy. Nineteen is *ridiculous*. Absolutely stupid. Believe me, I know, you don't have to tell me because I've told myself enough times. Say – how did we get on to this from the – the – subject we were talking about – what was that again?

The fact that you were involved in a relationship with her for a long time.

Oh, right.

Not a one-night stand.

If you're the one trying to be funny now, don't.

I'm not.

I thought you were making fun of it. If so I'll have to ask you to leave.

I – I wouldn't, Mr Wilmot. She was a lovely girl.

She was. Hey – you sound like you knew her.

I just meant – she looked lovely from the photograph in the paper.

Yeah, and plus it wasn't the kind of thing she would do, mock, humiliate. Take advantage. Quite a serious person, actually. Not boring, I don't mean that. Just that she thought about things. But look, right now I'm trying to remember about point three, back a while when we were talking about point three, or whatever, because I've got to keep on track now, I've got to get my life organised, I mean, I've ruined M's life, the kids, God only knows what else. And Anna with no job, the job was everything to her, I – I've got to concentrate on putting it all back together. Look, you've got me all confused now, would you mind leaving it for today? I – when I get confused I'm not good for much.

When shall I come back?

Oh, well, let's see – tomorrow, sure, make it tomorrow, I

usually clear things up in my mind pretty quickly and then I'm fine when it's a new day.

So: tomorrow will be a new day, Mr Wilmot. Aren't you a lucky man.

22

Well. Here we go again. Sorry about yesterday. I feel a lot better today, knew I would. Things always work that way for me, when things are tough, if I just get a little time off I'm fine. Hey – I hope you don't mind, but my folks will be coming over in a little while. In case there's anything you want to know from them.

Jackie's control is back. He has stopped drinking for almost a week and he has mastered Chuck. Nothing the lying scum can say will throw him off. Eventually he will hang himself.

Like what?

Well, they'll do anything to help me, so any angle you think maybe we haven't covered, you know, they'd be glad to get involved.

Obviously they already are.

Oh, yeah, they're very concerned, very loving. Mom doesn't think I know how to cook for myself so she comes by every other day with a 'Care' package. I don't say anything, I mean what's the point in hurting someone's feelings, and anyway, hey, she's a good cook. She picked out most of the furniture here, too, not that there was a lot to get for a place like this, but lucky for me she—

I wanted to ask you how Marilyn found out about the murder. That's an angle that comes to my mind. Speaking of angles.

Sure, fine, but you'll need to get a picture of my life here, the, uh, situation I'm in so to speak, to understand how M found out, my reactions to her finding out, etc., etc. Because if it wasn't for my mother I would have left this place the way it was, a dump, let's face it. And not exactly the neighbourhood I had in mind, but there isn't much you can afford without a job. Naturally I'm still paying the mortgage over at Levittown, or more to the point, Mom and Dad are lending me the money to pay it, so eventually when the kids come back, and hopefully me, too, everything will be squared away. We'll still have a place to go to, be a family again. So this is temporary, but Mom thought I should at least have a few chairs, a table, a bed, you know. Knives and forks. Why not? I'll pay them back when I get on my feet again, my father's keeping track, we go over the bills, I'm taking care of everything for Marilyn, and Dad takes care of this place, you know, rent, gas and electric, spending money for the week – no phone, he doesn't think a phone is all that necessary, which I tend to agree, you can't have everything in a situation like this. Phew. I'm wearing myself out. Where was I?

At home. Or so you said. Home at the time of her murder.

Oh, yeah, the kids, that's what I was about to say. I've mentioned before I have three kids, Bobby, Sally, and Ritchie, they're living at my parents' for the time being so there's all the expense of that, their upkeep, etc. And who knows? If this thing isn't resolved by the summer, there's camp, new sneakers, the works. Then bam, back to September, new clothes for school, books, you name it. Well, I can't believe we'll still be at this in September.

You figure all this will be over in no time.

Oh, Christ, I can't imagine living like this for ever. Thank God I have parents. Makes you wonder about poor people, doesn't it, who literally have nothing. I don't know how they manage. How they stand it. Being alone. Without support. That would be the worst.

I wonder.

Yuh, so to get back to your question, the one – say – is your coffee okay? Sorry I ran out of milk, I didn't get a chance to go out. I wasn't sure what time you were coming and I didn't want to be out when you got here. The alarm clock broke yesterday, boy, if it's not one thing it's another, and I asked Mom to bring me a new one. I have the radio but naturally they never say the time when you need it. I keep a list here for Mom, day-to-day things I run out of, might need, and then I give it to her.

I take it black.

Oh, right, yeah, now I remember. So.

How Marilyn found out.

The newspapers. Some of your crowd, the evening edition, and of course, what else, one of the busybody neighbours brought it over to M, the last thing she needed, and the kids heard the TV news that night. That's how the kids found out. What puzzles me is who could have told the papers that I knew her. Told the police. Jesus, I was so careful! Never went to her place. Well – a few times in the very beginning – but that was before anything happened. Nothing was going on, believe me, at that stage.

You mean sex?

Yes, I mean sex. What do *you* mean? What does anybody mean? Boy, you sure do have a way with words. Make the guy say it, that seems to be your motto. But, hey, this is what upsets me, I was so careful not to be seen with her, not to say anything. I just can't picture anybody thinking we knew each other the way we did. Outside work, I mean. Because occasionally we had to meet re. work, but I met lots of people every day, so nobody could have suspected anything, she would have just blended in with the normal business of the day. And we had agreed, during the day, strictly business. No looks, no special favours, nothing. The policy was, when other people are around, we don't know each other, end of story. When I was over with her boss and she was in and out with stuff, contracts, timetables, routing ledgers, whatever, that was it, nothing more. A job to be done. I know how to be professional and so does she.

Did.

Did, yuh, that's what I meant, she *did* know how to be a professional. She knew what we were up against.

Such as?

Rumours. Opinions. We had an agreement and we stuck to it: nobody but us will ever know about this.

But apparently something went very wrong, Mr Wilmot. How can you be so sure she didn't tell anyone?

I just am. I knew her. I trusted her completely. The deal was we said nothing to anyone about what was going on.

By the way. Just what *was* going on?

We were seeing each other! What do you think? We were – you know – hey, do you get a kick out of this? I hope somebody does. Intimate. On intimate terms. All right? Satisfied?

Not really. Something doesn't add up.

Oh. So now we're into mathematics.

I'm just wondering if you *had* said something to someone, or if by chance she had – which of course, as you point out, neither of you did – then what would it have been? Is that clear?

Clear? Oh, yeah, you're clear as a bell. Like for example I'd go up to my boss and say, Hello there, I'm betraying everything my family ever taught me, the trust of my wife and kids. Sure. Great. And now you'll probably ask me *why* again.

I might.

Why, why, why. You never get off that, do you? Regular one-track mind. At least you seem to agree I'm not basically that kind of guy, the kind of guy that breaks his word, that much I'll give you. 'So why did you do it?' the man keeps asking. Listen, if I were a psychiatrist, okay. Maybe. But don't make fun of me. You know I can't answer that.

So you can't answer why you got involved with her, you can't answer how somebody found out when you both agreed not to tell, you can't imagine who killed her, and you deny loving her. What *can* you account for, Mr Wilmot?

Hey! I'm aware of all those points, you don't stop making me aware of them. Despite me doing everything I could, someone found out. Obviously.

Which is interesting. Given your attention to detail.

You think that's interesting? Interesting isn't the word. What I wouldn't give to get my hands on whoever betrayed me because if it wasn't for that person, boy.

And how did *you* find out she was murdered?

I saw it in the early edition that morning. It was just a few sentences, you know – young woman discovered, cause of death unknown, tall, redhead, pretty, working at International Hauliers, studying at night, living at that address, name withheld, etc., etc.

You knew it was her?

Are you kidding? I knew right away.

You must have been shocked.

Ever see a cow struck by lightning? I saw that once. I don't recommend it. Huh. Funny I should say lightning.

Why?

Because that's what it felt like when I met her. And then again when I saw the paper. My first reaction was: at least she could have told me ahead of time so I didn't have to find out like this. Ridiculous! I read it, read it again. I thought there had to be a mistake somewhere. I actually phoned the paper and of course they confirmed the details. Very cagey, the guy on the phone, just like you. Only gave me what was in the paper. So then I phoned again ten minutes later, thought I might get a different person, but I got the same guy so I disguised my voice. You just call a minute ago? he barks. And I say, No, no, I just read this in the paper, I think I may have met this girl once, maybe you could just give me the first name, just to put my mind at ease, maybe I've got the wrong address. But no way. He wouldn't budge. Read the paper again, buddy, if you're so interested. Then he slammed down the phone. That was on the day itself. I – I, then later on Marilyn arrived at the office. Just before five, she was in the city shopping, I couldn't concentrate on anything. I thought of going to her apartment, but I couldn't risk being seen, being identified, I mean, what if the cops thought I did it?

They do.

Exactly. So I just sat in my office, I tried to sit, I paced, when suddenly there's M coming through the door. I had just been thinking to myself, maybe I'll chance it, I could pretend I'm someone else, pretend I'm at the building to visit someone else, if I could just get someone to verify that it was her, or wasn't, and if it was, then maybe with luck I'd get to see the body and then I'd believe it, I still don't believe it, or maybe she'd come out of the building and say it was all a big mistake. Chuck, she'd say – now, you have to understand, I wasn't thinking straight, normally I know what I'm doing – Chuck, they thought I was murdered! Isn't that amazing! But I'm not murdered, I'm alive! I'll meet you at our spot at five thirty—

'Our spot?'

A rooming house with a bar downstairs called the No Name. Third Avenue. Funny place, lopsided, seen better days I suppose you'd have to admit. Run down. But it was *ours*.

Anyone ever know about it?

No. No one outside. The barmen, the staff, they understood, we were safe. So it was ideal. We'd sit there for hours. Then go upstairs to our little room. But I still – I – it's a funny thing – I have things to *tell* her. Things I have to say, I just, there wasn't the time to say certain things.

What things?

That's just it, I don't know. If she showed up right now, even then I probably wouldn't know. I'm actually losing sleep over this, this something I have to tell her, whatever it is. I lie awake wracking my brain, I go over and over what I *did* tell her to see if I left anything out, and I'll be damned, I can't think of one thing that didn't get said. All about my parents, the Navy, Marilyn, and the kids. A lot about the business, we had a lot in common on that, of course, and there are some big developments coming up which we discussed in detail. You probably wouldn't understand. New legislation in connection with taxes on exports, shipping will be affected, not the import side so much but—

So she knew how to listen.

Listen? Oh, brother. She could really listen.

And Marilyn?

See, Marilyn and I don't talk much any more. I suppose after fourteen years everything is just about covered, and well—

Marilyn doesn't listen.

To be honest with you, no. Marilyn does not listen. I'm not criticising. Just saying.

Why do you think that is?

I have a few theories about it. One: her parents don't listen, so she probably got it from them. Two: and if you've met her you'll know what I mean, she drinks too much.

Which I'm not happy about and which I told her when I moved out, I'm not coming back if you don't do something about it. Dry out or whatever they do.

So you figure she has a problem.

Reality. She can't face reality. But don't get me wrong: I love her. I see her for who she is and I accept her. My love for her has never changed.

So you loved Marilyn throughout the four years of your relationship with the girl – who you did not love.

Right. You could say that.

You are the one saying it, Mr Wilmot. I am the one finding it hard to believe.

Hey. That's not my problem, *Mr* Molloy, if you want to be so formal about it. I am telling you how it was. You gripe when I can't answer the questions and now you gripe when I can.

But you have all these complaints about Marilyn. And you had another relationship. You must have needed something.

Yeah, well, okay, I see what you mean. I was even feeling guilty the other day, wondering if maybe I took up most of our time—

With Marilyn?

No. The other relationship. My needs. Like you were saying. We never had a lot of time. Mind you, she was a great talker herself. And I didn't mind. Whereas with M. I mind. On the other hand, in the, uh, situation I had with the young lady, well, she might have had a tendency to be a bit, what would you call it, hyperactive. Had to be slowed down, used to get quite excited. Sex! Boy! Well, she was young, that was the thing, whereas Marilyn is more of a mature person, I never have to tell Marilyn to slow down in the sex department. The other girl used to get carried away. Also with ideas about the future.

Yours and hers?

Yeah. How we'd be in love for ever and all that. She even wanted to go to *Marilyn*, get everything out in the open! Me get a divorce! God! Can you imagine?

Oh, yes. I can.

So in other words, not putting too fine a point on it, she said she loved me, she actually used that word. Which was part of the being romantic for her. She liked that. Oh, I suppose I'm as romantic as the next guy, why not? But carried away? The whole idea makes me laugh! A grown man? We're not kids any more, nobody'd get anything done. That's what I tried to explain to her, but she thought anything was possible if you just wanted it enough. I'm not saying she was *unbalanced* or anything like that, but I would say, yes, that she was more on the throw-caution-to-the-wind side of things. Whereas me, I'm a batten-down-the-hatches type of person. I'm not saying *never*, I'm saying when you know what's what, when you've got all your ducks in a row, okay, *then* go to it, let go all you want.

And when would that ever be, Mr Wilmot?

Funny. I just realised that's what I did in the Navy. Batten down the hatches. I was known for it. Matter of life and death. She used to tease me. She'd say, Come on, the Navy days are over, nobody's checking up on you, everything doesn't have to be so tight. Whereas of course in the Navy, on a ship, Christ, every little detail has to be right. Where was I?

That question again.

Oh, yeah, that she talked, too, I wasn't the only one, so I shouldn't feel guilty, she had a lot of things going on—

Wait a minute – what things?

In her life. Different situations.

But what *were* they, Mr Wilmot? You're not telling me anything, you might be holding back something important.

It's none of your business! Everyone has things going on,

for Christ sake. She was no different. She needed a friend, she needed to talk.

But you still haven't said about *what.* How many times do I have to ask?

And you haven't said why you want to know! Oh, I can see you're sitting on the edge of the chair now all right, something's got you going and I'm beginning to wonder what it is, why you're so goddamn curious and why you never say how any of this will help me. *Me.* The guy heading for the electric chair. Remember him? I thought we were doing each other a favour. So where's your favour to me? What are *you* giving? Ever occur to you maybe some stuff isn't your business? That you can't just march into the shop and grab things off the shelves? What went on in her life is *private.* What she told me is *private.*

What's happened, Jackie? Where's the control? You're going down, you're slipping. Stop! Get out, leave, hold on to the chair, the table, anything!

Good. Now *you're* the one getting agitated. Find out what it's like to be under a hot light. But it's only a goddamn story, isn't it. Nothing to you. Go ahead. Get up and pace. You don't have to answer to me, you don't have to answer to anybody. Oh, I see, and now you go through the cupboards, just like that, don't bother asking, it's only my *home,* even if it is a dump, sure, go ahead, slam the doors. If you're looking for booze you won't find any in there. Guess where I keep it? Go into my bedroom, a big bottle of wine on the floor by the bed, the kind they drink down on the Bowery. Don't worry, my mother keeps me supplied, have all you want. Found it? Feeling better? Some interview. Some way to clear my name, the reporter guzzling rot gut in the subject's apartment. Your paper know about you, Mr Molloy?

Actually I'm glad you're not talking. True silence is beautiful. How about sharing some of my wine with me? A little drinky-poo for Charles J. Wilmot III, Mr Nice Guy. I'm beginning to think we have something in common, Molloy. What – I can't imagine. But here we are. Me, I feel just great. I haven't given anybody a piece of my mind in years. Oh, Christ, there's the doorbell. Must be the folks. All right, all right!

I'll go – I – this shouldn't have happened.

No – sit down, stay right where you are, Molloy. I'm beginning to enjoy this. Coming, Mom! Give me the bottle, I'll put it back where it belongs.

23

14 February 1959. Jackie is following the girl. She has just left her office, one hour earlier than usual, four p.m. Twenty-sixth Street between Third and Lexington, International Hauliers, a huge building of grey stone. Jackie arrived in time, suspecting. Wondering where she might go. Who she might meet on Valentine's Day.

208 East 26th Street faces a row of similar grey or brown stone edifices, twenty or twenty-five storeys, blocks wedged together to make a fortress wall. Both sides of 26th are lined with these monstrosities, creating a black tunnel that suffocates sunlight.

Jackie yawns and bundles his coat up to his chin. Pulls his Greek sailor's cap down over his forehead on to his eyebrows. The ship *Mykonos* is docked in New York Harbor for a week . . .

As the girl turns the corner on to Third Avenue, she stops for a moment to observe herself in a shop window. She is wearing make-up and the scratches underneath have nearly healed. She enters a card shop.

Jackie does the same and watches her browse through Valentines. His mind wanders. He picks up a card, roses are red, as the girl borrows a pen from the man behind the counter and writes inside the card she has purchased. She finishes, returns the pen, slips the card into its envelope and then into her handbag.

Routine. At last. Just a story, any story. Events in the No Name and at 143 Farmyard Lane are long ago, past tense. Jackie Molloy is good at that, shifting experience from front to back, now to then, forgotten. The shell game: now you see, now you don't, and so it is that he can become a Greek sailor touring New York. She won't see me, won't recognise, won't remember. I am nowhere near.

The girl leaves the shop. Jackie follows. No doubt she will meet Chuck at the No Name. Jackie is back at work, hard at work, and no doubt during these last two weeks when he has done nothing else, they have been there often. So what? Of no consequence, just another once-upon-a-time. After today I'm finished: promoted. Marty's been overruled, I'm going to Washington. They can all rot. Why am I even bothering today? Is this my farewell? My Valentine? Jackie showing Jackie he got away? Yes. Nobody traps Mick Molloy's son, he's one step ahead, one step up, and from now on he'll be in Washington with the big boys. In the know. He'll watch and listen and he'll have what everybody wants and they'll come to him to buy what he's got: secrets.

The girl stops at the corner of 29th and Third. Opens her bag and reaches in. She turns, still searching the bag. Jackie pretends to study the window of a souvenir shop. Makes sure his collar is shielding the side of his face as he strains his eyes to catch her.

Rummaging. Uneasy. Looking left and right. Is she being followed? Of course, you fool: she is being followed by *you*. But she cannot know that.

She starts to walk back in the direction from which she has come. Perhaps she left something in the office. Perhaps the gift that is to go with the card. She is worried that she will now be late for her date with Chuck.

Give her a moment to pass. Then let her go. Let her walk toward the awaiting fate. Hers, not yours. She looks perfectly fine today, no ill effects, Chuck will take care of her. As she passes, you may gaze at her fading relevance, and this gaze will mark the end of her existence meeting yours.

Jackie turns to watch the departing. Not a girl: a thought, an image. Idea of a person.

But, no. She has not gone. Has not walked away as Jackie had instructed.

Rather, she is facing the Greek sailor, working her lips as only she can in the mewl of longing to be found. With a laboured smile she comes forward. Jackie is paralysed, a deer caught in the headlights. For in her outstretched hand is the Valentine.

Please.

Jackie, a statue.

She starts to panic.

Please.

Stone.

She flees. She places the red envelope on the shelf inside a phone booth and runs on.

This red the only living breathing presence on Third Avenue. Glaring, blaring, light and siren, nee-na, nee-na, Georgie, Georgie, Jackie, Jackie, where a-a-are you?

Jackie walks past the phone booth. No longer in the existing.

The girl must have gone. There was a girl here but she is not here now so she must have gone. Oh, well. Or perhaps there was no girl. Yes, that must be it. No girl at all.

For several blocks Jackie strolls. Studies shop windows. Nice day for a walk. Almost five o'clock.

He hasn't eaten since breakfast. He sighs. Thought begins to return. Normality. He reviews recent events.

The meeting with Marty and the Washington Bureau Chief, euphoria at watching Marty fight to own him and lose. He gorged himself on Marty's defeat and forgot about food. Jackie had agreed to the transfer just to savour that moment. Had watched and listened and angled behind Marty's back. To make sure the offer arrived just when Marty needed him most.

Now Jackie feels hungry. I've shed Marty, the girl, all of them. I'll stop and have a sandwich. Then home and organise for Washington. Say goodbye to Frank and Joanne, maybe go back to the office for a few more files. At last: the pieces where they belong.

A coffee shop in the next block. Jackie enters, breathes deeply, freely. Where to sit, a simple decision. A chair with a table? A stool at the counter? Jackie is filled with pleasure at his return to the rudiments.

No, Jackie. No.

Simplicity is not to be. Not to be the dissolution of auras.

Out of the corner of your eye, her coat.

She is removing her cap, shaking out the bountiful hair. At a table for four. She is about to sit down at a table for four nearly hidden in the corner, camouflaged by other customers bunched at surrounding tables. And two people are already seated at this table, waiting for her.

Jackie is a still and floating presence. Not located in this world of chairs, tables, earth. The angle is poor, the coffee shop crowded, but as he hovers like a gas, there and not there, observing but invisible, he has no doubt that the girl is about to sit down with two people.

Jackie twists and bends, can make out two sets of feet under the table. Women's shoes, both pairs. Where before? Vague recollection guides Jackie back to substance.

All he can make out above ground is the girl's head, the back of her head, and she is not being welcomed. A voice is raised.

Sound, Jackie. Sight. Awake.

The people blocking Jackie's view start to clear away. And in the clearing—

What is it, Jackie?

Impossible. Cannot be.

Oh, but it is.

I won't see.

You do see.

Not the yearned-for demise of association after all. Jackie's attempt on the conscious life has failed.

For Anna Laskowski and Marilyn Wilmot are seated with the girl.

Anna Laskowski and Marilyn Wilmot who are not supposed to know her.

But do know.

And there is a subject of great and serious interest between them that has been spoken of before. No introductions, no hesitation, seamless understanding weaving them together.

You have no idea what the meeting is about. No idea how or why these women have been brought together.

Nor the reason Anna Laskowski has now produced a brown-paper bag from which she takes and then places in the centre of the table a belt. She and Marilyn stare at this object. The girl holds her head and cannot look.

The blood red of the Valentine gathers speed and builds to a roar. The train is leaving. Keep up, can't keep up.

Must.

Remain in the life of solids, Jackie. But how?

No!

You and this story are over, you are going to Washington. Your own journey. A fate apart. Loosen your hold, release the screaming vehicle. Just leave the snaking maze of tracks, signals and announcements, go back to the station and start again. After the first roll of the dice simply go a different way. Nothing *has* to be.

Self-determination. Free will.

Go.

Sugar bowls, knives forks spoons, glasses of water.

Well, excuse *me*, aren't *we* in a hurry.

Hey, you! Hey, buddy! Come back here!

Aw, Christ sake, Joe, he don't speak English, they fuckin' come over here and can't even talk the fuckin' language and fuckin' destroy the place.

The place, the place, where was it, which way?

Huffing and puffing blow the house down, Jackie Molloy rounds the bend. Knees quivering, buckling, he grabs the man talking on the phone and hauls him out of the booth.

Too late.

The bent and broken metal shelf.

No red, no life, no word.

The Valentine is gone.

24

Same same, over and over. Swiftly pass the waters.

Down-river suction, upstream resistance, this is Jackie Molloy: clutching sandbars, illusion of middle ground. Exhausting himself against the inclination of currents.

Jackie opens his eyes, sits up, and says to Miguelito, sparkling champagne of hypnosis: It is not true that I couldn't figure Chuck out.

What did you figure out about him, Molloy?

Jackie begins to weep. The tears slide backward and run slowly down the lines of his chin. In silence pass the waters.

Jackie replies: Don't make me go back.

No, Molloy, you can't make somebody, and Miguelito helps Jackie lie down again.

I'll talk to Chuck. Chuck again, that's what to do. Not Anna. Please not Anna.

Listen to me, Molloy: what you figure out about this guy? And Anna? Huh?

Not Anna, no.

You keep saying her name to go away. But that mean she on you doorstep. Go on, go to the door. She can't hurt you here.

Oh, yes: hurt. Journeys from here to there are long, and make no promises. And yet, on Miguelito's table in a room wafting with freshly washed cotton, Jackie Molloy boards the bus again for 141st Street in Astoria, then takes the E train four stops to 179th and Queens Boulevard.

You look exhausted, Mr Molloy. May I get you a drink of water?

The interviews are on the decline. The interviews Jackie does not want to remember. When the possibility of escape was collapsing. Like Jackie Molloy, a house of cards.

No. I'm fine.

You do not appear fine. Have you been in some difficulty?

I told you I'm all right. I'd like to begin.

When you did not arrive on the day we had agreed for our last appointment I phoned your newspaper and spoke to someone called Marty. He said there was no excuse for your breaking the appointment without contacting me and I agreed. As I suspected, he said you have done this kind of thing before. He told me he has even gone to the trouble of having your research department provide information for you on the unfortunate manner of the girl's death, and you have refused to read it. Not a very responsible way to approach a serious situation.

Why don't we just get to the point, Miss Laskowski. I'm here now.

Whatever the point *is*. I am beginning to wonder.

You know what the point is. We both do.

I am afraid I wasn't much help the last time we spoke. Being unsure of the point to which you refer.

Oh, you were a big help and I know you will be today.

How kind of you to say so, Mr Molloy. And now, as we proceed, I will ask you to keep your voice down. My parents are sleeping.

Just begin, Miss Laskowski.

Why don't you start with what you need to know? I believe that would be the usual format.

You think this is a usual case?

I have no experience of crime, Mr Molloy. However, I imagine the police have dealt with murder before, yes.

Strangulation.

That is the method. Not the case itself.

Really? I can assure you strangulation is more than a technique. Perhaps you would like to see photographs.

As you might expect, Mr Molloy, I am not acquainted with the seamier side of life. Thank goodness. Apparently you are. However, I am quite aware that elements of darkness exist in everyone and I am quite capable of realising that people would enjoy violating each other.

Enjoy? Did you say enjoy?

Of course. Surely you are not so naive as to believe that people feel badly when they are destructive to others. They enjoy it. Why else would they do it?

Perhaps for the same reasons some of them lie. Just as you are now.

I beg your pardon?

You. Right now.

How very interesting. When I myself am aware only of telling the truth. Perhaps you would be kind enough to reveal what it is I am lying about, Mr Molloy.

Don't play games, Miss Laskowski. We both know you're lying.

Games? Oh, no, this is not a game. The penalty for murder is the electric chair. The outcome of that procedure is probably no less attractive than the results of strangulation.

I'm sure the police have told you you'll have a good chance of avoiding it if you tell the truth.

And *you* would avoid a lot of unpleasantness, too, Mr

Molloy, if *you* were to tell the truth. Therefore when you outline for me what I am lying about, perhaps you would also clarify something else.

Yes?

The matter of how you, a supposed stranger to me, can possibly know more about what I am saying than I do myself. That is another mystery. How such a situation might come about.

We are not here to talk about me. I have nothing to do with it.

Oh, really?

You are twisting things around to avoid answering my questions.

Oh, no, Mr Molloy. That is what *you* are doing. And wouldn't it be nice to know why. Because for the most part I find you very patient and understanding. In turn, I am giving you and the police whatever you ask. I trust I do not need to say that I feel it is my duty to co-operate with an official investigation into the commission of a serious crime. I realise that may sound naive to some, but this is what I believe. Perhaps I am more conscientious than most—

Most suspects.

Pardon me?

Suspects. You are a prime suspect, Miss Laskowski, and for good reason.

Yes. I am a suspect. Of course I am aware of that, and that is what I am trying to explain, that perhaps most suspects would not have my particular background. An executive secretary is trained to be objective, impartial. Free of her own viewpoint. Which permits great authority in observation. Inner strength, a sense of what is right and what is wrong, is essential. A secretary is often in the middle of – how shall I say it – confidential activities and discussions – and one could, unwittingly, become drawn into these matters. Tempted. But one should not give in. The reporter's dilemma, no doubt. The dilemma of someone who prefers to stand back and watch. And yet unexpectedly finds himself getting involved. Isn't that how we might describe it, Mr Molloy?

I have nothing to do with this story, Miss Laskowski.

Please, Mr Molloy. I am not stupid.

You are the one who got drawn in. You helped Mr Wilmot phone his lover. And you are not telling me why.

I would not consider placing his calls to this to girl to have been participation.

What would you call it?

Any word will do, Mr Molloy. I know I did not participate. I also know that the police find the fact that I placed those calls very interesting. But I had no idea who he was phoning, did I? I was completely ignorant of the identity of the other party and of the details of Mr Wilmot's private life. I have tried to be honest in saying – because I don't want all of you to get your hopes up in regard to what I have to contribute to the investigation, the story – that all I can report are the facts of Mr Wilmot's daily schedule at the office, and my own. I told the police quite clearly that this is all I know about. And yet, they still insist that I might have been party to the violent act in question. I can only repeat that I know what I know and what I do not know. One is this and one is that, separate and distinct, each in its proper place.

How very neat.

Yes. And this is precisely why I cannot understand your deep concern about this story, Mr Molloy. For you do care, oh, yes, my goodness, that much is clear to me. But I keep asking myself what possible reason there might be and I have no answer. Why a person who should be separate and distinct, he in his place, I in mine, is not staying where he belongs. Could it be – and no doubt I am completely wrong even to suggest such a possibility – could it be that *you* are the one playing games? The one, if I may be so blunt, who is lying?

You are very clever, Miss Laskowski.

Oh, heavens, no. I am just myself. Only what I appear. Whereas you – yes, this is it – you are not what you appear to be, Mr Molloy. If only I knew why. And what your deception has to do with me.

Ah, silence. So you *are* interested. I was right.

Of course I am. In your help. And you are helping me a lot.

I am so glad to be of assistance.

Did you ever see Mr Wilmot outside the office?

Of course not. Why would we? We had a professional relationship.

The police believe you met him on a number of occasions. They even think you knew the girl.

Ridiculous.

Naturally. That would be impossible.

Yes, it would. And I am surprised they relay these accusations through you.

You feel accused?

I do not *feel* accused, Mr Molloy. I *am* accused. A simple fact. Even you, for reasons, as I say, I have not yet discovered, speak to me in an accusatory manner. Everyone does these days. Shopkeepers I have known for years.

You do or say nothing that would dispel doubts about you, Miss Laskowski.

Why should I? I am innocent. It is not my job to help you and the police. I owe none of you anything. All of you break your promises. First the police say they will protect me, then they try to build a case against me. You come along promising a series of articles on the human side of tragedy, a series you assure me will give a balanced view of a complex situation and probably help to vindicate me once my voice is heard. So far you have not produced one word. So tell us the truth, Mr Molloy – you claim to be interested in truth, don't you – there isn't going to be a series, is there? That is not really why you are here.

You bitch. Answer the questions.

My, my. Truth is not such an easy subject after all. The man at the *Mirror* did mention your temper. And alcohol. Would you like a drink? Scotch, isn't it?

I don't need a drink. Let's get on with this.

Oh, I insist. You haven't looked well since you came in, Mr Molloy. Quite clearly something is bothering you, upsetting you. It must be hard to work in such a state. You mustn't be able to concentrate properly. Excuse me – where are you going? Mr Molloy!

Where's the bathroom? Where is it!

Down the hall to the left. Please. Do try to keep the noise down. Noise is not necessary.

Now. Is that better? Do you like ice with your Scotch?

Don't think you'll be able to distract me.

Relax, Mr Molloy. I'm happy to answer all your questions, you'll get your story. I'll put the bottle and the ice bucket right here beside you, just help yourself.

Go back over the schedule. The schedule that day. And don't change the subject.

Fine. I told you he left the office. No one knows why, or where he went. I was most incorrect to suggest he went out in order to make his telephone calls. The police were very curious about my saying that, and for some reason I think you are, too. Even though I keep telling everyone that this comment was just my own speculation, nothing more. Nothing to do with reality. But everyone keeps saying, isn't it interesting you would think of that, of all possibilities, that he might be going out to phone this girl.

It's a fair question, Miss Laskowski. Why would Mr

Wilmot feel the need to go out to call her when he had already been asking you to put him through from the office? Why would you, therefore, even think it?

Yes, yes, of course. What I suggested makes no sense at all. I would make a terrible detective.

And yet you are so precise and logical. That's what interests me. That your idea is completely illogical.

Well, there we are, Mr Molloy: I am a human being.

Even you make mistakes.

Exactly. And as for you, you seem suddenly to be feeling much better. Your questions are sharper, your concentration restored. I am so glad. Do help yourself to some more Scotch.

I appreciate the refreshment, Miss Laskowski. But I can assure you that my concentration is only part of the job. And you are only the subject of a story. Nothing more. My professionalism demands that I keep my distance and I do.

So I have heard. You have won some awards with your 'distance'. I, however, have yet to experience it.

What time of day did he go out, Miss Laskowski?

Morning. Didn't I say it was morning? I meant to. Before lunch. He was in the office by himself all afternoon, from 12.30, until, as I said, Mrs Wilmot arrived at ten minutes to five. He had a sandwich and coffee at his desk, a ham sandwich, which he brought in himself, and I fixed him a coffee from the trolley, extra milk and two sugars. He had the meal at his desk with the door closed.

Was that a problem, Mrs Wilmot arriving? I mean, I presume business was essentially over for the day.

Ten minutes to five is still normal working hours, Mr Molloy. The fact that it would be nearly five is not the point. Often there is some considerable work to be done at the end of the day, and this might, in fact, be when the pressure on Mr Wilmot and me is the most intense. I do not criticise Mrs Wilmot for this, but it has been her habit to arrive from time to time unexpectedly, as she did that day, just as we are trying to tie up loose ends, review the day's business, urgent matters in many cases, tomorrow's schedule, and so on.

Where would you and Mr Wilmot meet for your discussions?

In his office. We generally conduct our conferences at the end of the day in his office.

With the door closed?

Certainly the door would be closed. I do not like your implication. There is no need for that sort of speculation which you know yourself is beyond the bounds of reality.

Did you ever wonder why Mrs Wilmot chose to arrive when she did? On that day.

No. Why would I? When she comes is her prerogative.

Maybe she suspected Mr Wilmot of having an affair and wanted to be sure he came straight home after work.

How would I know? Good heavens. I suppose in theory, yes, in theory she could have known of, suspected, he was having an affair with that girl. How – that is another question. I certainly do not keep track of Mrs Wilmot. And as to your implication that she may have worried about *my* intentions with Mr Wilmot, well, I think you are letting the police influence your better judgement, such as it is. One must be careful not to descend to the level below.

Something is puzzling me. Perhaps you could just refresh my memory on the sequence of events after Mrs Wilmot arrived on the 14th.

Yes. Sequence of events. Let's see now. I remember telling you the girl at the switch buzzed me at my desk to say Mrs Wilmot was coming, and then I saw her, said hello – oh. I see what you are getting at. How silly of me. I have now told you we were in his office in conference, while before I told you I was at my desk. I've been – I – yes, well, there have been so many questions. Perhaps – wouldn't it be possible that I have become slightly confused? Let me think for a moment. I am sure I will remember the way it actually was – it – uh, yes, do you think this is important? If so, *why* is it important? All days in an office are very much alike, perhaps that is the difficulty. I told the police everything I could and I have told you – of course, if I happened to be in Mr Wilmot's office when Mrs Wilmot arrived, I would return to my desk immediately. That is the proper protocol. So she could be private with him. That must be what happened – I was in both places, so to speak.

Amazing. Two places at once. How did you feel about her arrival?

Feel? I am not sure I follow you.

Do try, Miss Laskowski. What's happened to all your confidence about the truth? How did Mrs Wilmot's arrival affect you that day? It's a simple question.

Well, certainly any interruption in the middle of business puts back the timing of things.

You mean she was interfering.

An interference, yes, if you want to use that word. With the day's business activity. At those times. On the few days, the rare occasions, that she came. I would not want to generalise. Nor judge another person.

But why that day? She didn't come every day. Why that day of all days did she come, and why that day did you feel she was interfering?

I have no idea why that day as opposed to any other. You keep going at me and at me over this one minor point. I never knew what made her choose the days she chose. I suppose it is just an accident she happened to come in on the same day as this girl was found murdered. Apparently you don't believe in accidents.

No, I don't.

But *I* do. And I am not judging Mrs Wilmot for interfering. She did not know it was interference. Anyway, that was *your* word, not mine. You made me say it. In fact, I've always liked Mrs Wilmot.

Liked her?

In general. As one would any person.

Really?

Why wouldn't I? I respect her. She has a right to come in to her own husband's office.

Had. He's been fired. And they've separated.

Yes, yes, there you go again, of course that's what I meant. Now that he's been let go, I – she – well, the whole situation does not apply, it is a different situation. Something else. Life moves on.

You forgot to say you've been fired, too.

Oh, didn't I mention I've been let go? Obviously you already knew it anyway. Yes. Now that Mr and Mrs Wilmot and I are being accused, I've been let go.

So your actions have had consequences.

I see you are trying a different approach now. You have given up on my lies – which you cannot name – and moved on to my actions. Perhaps you would enlighten me as to what those actions were, Mr Molloy, even if you cannot pin down the lies. After you finish pouring your third drink, that is.

You don't want to talk about losing your job, do you? You didn't expect that. You never thought you'd be accused. You think the police are stupid. In fact, you have nothing but contempt for just about everybody.

If you don't mind, Mr Molloy. A young woman has been cruelly murdered and I am sure she would rather we stay on the main point and do our best to apprehend her killer. Rather than try our hand at psychology. The main point at the moment is that one would not allow the firm's reputation to be called into question. I would have resigned had they not approached me first. That goes without saying for someone with my experience.

Pardon me – my throat is a bit dry. I'll just get a glass of water.

There. And you, Mr Molloy – what's started you sneezing? Do you have a cold?

Funny – as you walked back to the chair – an aroma—

We seem to get on quite well when we settle down and relax, don't we? I am beginning to think we might even come to understand one another.

There's no understanding here, Miss Laskowski.

Oh, I don't agree, Mr Molloy. I am sure that if you give some thought to the situation we are both in – as I have been doing since you arrived – you will discover what I might be referring to.

It sounds as if I shouldn't have mentioned your being fired. You've changed the subject again, trying to talk about *me*.

Not at all. You are the one who seems upset. And I am sure I do not need to tell you, Mr Molloy, that emotion has no place in this. It will only take you off the track, make you unable to do what needs to be done.

Obviously I pushed you too hard. Fine. I'll go then.

Oh, no. Please stay. I find this conversation most enlightening. Perhaps you find me difficult to understand. My parents' values and ideals are not, well, perhaps not American. A way of thinking that would be simpler and easier for you to comprehend. My parents have what the uninformed would consider old-fashioned ideas. One's first obligation is not to oneself or to passing moments of temporary feeling – first there is loyalty. Commitment. Co-operation and joint effort are more important than the fleeting impulse of one individual. Some people have a tendency to laugh at rules. My parents and I do not. You are shocked at my reaction to Mrs Wilmot, aren't you? Shocked that I am so accepting of her. And at the same time so uninterested. No doubt you are a modern person and do not understand that kind of discipline. Mrs Wilmot is one person and I am another. There is, there was, no connection between us. She is over there, I am here. Distinct. No mixing up.

Culture is one thing, Miss Laskowski, but you *were* connected with Mrs Wilmot. Very definitely.

Why do you insist upon saying that? I had nothing whatever to do with her.

Of course you did.

She was nothing to me.

Nothing except *Mr* Wilmot.

Mr Wilmot, obviously. You are stating the obvious. We both had a relationship with him, yes. Well – I don't know. I would not have referred to it that way. A word *you* would use, relationship.

You spent a lot of time together. I would call that a relationship.

That much is true. Time. It is a lot of time to spend with a person. More than he spent at home – not that he *preferred* the office, no, just out of necessity. We worked together hours and hours every day, sometimes weekends.

You spent weekends working with Mr Wilmot?

Certainly. I imagine even you are capable of working weekends, Mr Molloy, when there is something urgent. Of course I would go in when asked. What did I just say about commitment?

And your parents? Who would take care of them?

The woman across the hall. She looks in on them during the week and fixes their lunch if I have to work on Saturday or Sunday. They are not big eaters, and I prepare everything in advance without salt or fats. Fish, chicken, vegetables, oatmeal. It is not complicated, everything is in place for them. And I always phoned. Three times a day. Ten o'clock, two o'clock, and again just as I was leaving the office. Never later than five forty-five. And I am very careful these days about making them take their nap. The police in and out, all of us giving statements, this has tired them.

The one thing I'm still wondering about is how you knew the girl.

I didn't! How could I have known such a person! You and the police are collaborating! They even think I bought a belt like one Mrs Wilmot owns to make it look as though *she* committed the crime. When would I have time for all that? I catch the E train at ten minutes past seven, the first bus at seven thirty-five, the second at eight fifteen, and as I have already mentioned, I am in the office by eight forty-five, sometimes eight thirty depending on traffic, and everyone in that office – go ahead, ask them, I have nothing to fear – everyone knows my comings and goings, there is a certain way I would conduct myself and they all know it. Accounts Payable, Accounts Receivable, Marketing, Purchasing – ask them. They all know me, they all know my schedule never varies. Perhaps a free-lancer does not realise that the true value of an employee lies in his or her consistency, perhaps in journalism this quality is not so important, but for a person of standing in my profession it is, the doing each day of things that must be done. Real things, Mr Molloy. Real things to a set standard. A predictable, reliable standard.

So tell me about her. This girl.

Why do you keep coming back to her! Stay away from her!

Now we see who's getting emotional. You don't want me mentioning that girl, do you? She's a time bomb, ticking away inside you.

I am not upset. Merely frustrated. I am doing my best to help you. I too want the facts kept in order and I am quite sure of the sequence of events for any given day and certainly, although there might be, could be, variation, I would try to guard against it, naturally, because variation would confuse procedures, but I realise that change can and does occur in life and I would happily adapt to that change.

Okay. Have it your way. I can assure you, you've given me all the information I need. But since you're so interested in variation, tell me what you think caused the variation that day.

Back to that day, that day, will people ever stop talking about that day?

What other day is there any more, Miss Laskowski?

Let me answer your question! Give me a moment!

Oh, by all means. Take your time.

Now. I suppose different things may have caused variation in the schedule. Unexpected telephone calls. Telegrams. In any case, they were minor. To the best of my recollection.

But your parents told the police you didn't phone at the usual times that day. And on the 13th, they say you left early to go into work – a Sunday no less – and phoned in the afternoon to say that the neighbour would be giving them dinner. Apparently you were going out at the end of the day. I wonder where.

My parents' memory is not always the best. And the policeman who translated their Polish was, well, how shall I say it nicely: not up to the task. So both those reports were incorrect.

So their memory, and the police, failed them.

Exactly.

My goodness, Mr Molloy. Sneezing again.

Did you spray something in here? What is that fragrance?

Really, Mr Molloy. Have you seen me use a spray?

Never mind, never mind. Look, Miss Laskowski: how do you explain that the weekend cleaning woman at your office reported overhearing the conversation of the 13th in which you told your parents you would not be home that evening? And that according to one of the other secretaries you did in fact leave the office more than once on the 14th?

The secretary in question on the 14th, well – I was ill, briefly, last year and she had dearly hoped to replace me as Mr Wilmot's secretary. She and her boss, Head of Purchasing, were in on it together. And as to that cleaning woman: she is deaf.

The cleaning woman is deaf. There is an explanation for everything.

Indeed.

Were you the more senior to the secretary you mention?

Yes. Mr Wilmot is senior to Purchasing, which is senior to Maintenance.

What was the problem?

He tried to undermine Mr Wilmot. He openly questioned his decisions in front of top management. In meetings he challenged, in particular, his handling of the International Hauliers account, and I can tell you personally that we handled that account impeccably.

The girl's company.

She had no connection with our business, Mr Molloy. With the important dealings that took place between ABC and International.

If you didn't know her, how can you know that?

I just know.

Perhaps Mr Wilmot was losing his objectivity because of his relationship with her.

No, Mr Molloy. Mr Wilmot and I do not lose objectivity. You are the one who suffers from that difficulty. The Head of Purchasing and his secretary simply resented Mr Wilmot and me. But they had no cause for antagonism. There is nothing personal about organisational structure. We are over Purchasing and that is just the way it is. The levels did not take their coffee together, that would not have been right. Nor would I have initiated communication with her. It would be up to her, being beneath me, to initiate. To come to me if she needed something. She found these structures difficult to accept, she had ideas about her future. I am not judging the girl, anyone is entitled to improve themselves.

So she would have reason to make up stories about you. In order to get rid of you.

Exactly. She would be happy to tell the police I had left the office when I had not.

But the others confirmed her version of events.

Isn't the answer to that obvious? She is friends with the others. They would all tell the same story.

Ah, yes. Of course. How silly of me to think there might be a loose end. And when was your last day?

I was given notice the day after Mr Wilmot. I was shown to the lift by the Head of Personnel who thanked me for my years of service. However, as I am sure you would agree, these are not important issues, considering that someone has been murdered. These are simply questions of structure and procedure. Why ever do you bother so much about details?

I don't. *You* do. You've lost your job, Miss Laskowski. Everything. Not what you planned.

You have the impression that I care about details? But I am not suggesting any such interest, I am merely answering your questions as requested. *You* are raising the matter of my job.

Consequences, Miss Laskowski. Your lies and your actions have come back to haunt you.

Don't talk to me about lies! Who are *you*? Do you ever face the truth about yourself?

I haven't committed murder, Miss Laskowski.

As if *I* have! There you go again, you've taken us way off the point! You're always mixing one thing up with another, one person with another – Mrs Wilmot with me and now you with me – I cannot understand how a person with so little sense of order can write a story.

Consequences, consequences, bills come due.

Here – take a tissue. Yes. The last day was the 16th. The Personnel Manager walked me to the lift and then I came home. Came home. Now see here, Mr Molloy, I think we should stop this. We're just going around and around. The same details. The way things got accomplished, how the day was, nothing that will tell anyone very much.

Oh! Mama! Papa! What are you doing awake? It's not time yet. Go back in your room right now.

No, he is not the police. Not sick, he's fine. A nice man who will help us.

They want to sit with us and have a drink while I tell you about my education.

I've already heard about your fucking education. I'm leaving. Goodbye.

Good riddance! You want truth from me and *you* come with lies? Get out.

A pleasure.

Oh, that is what you say, but you'll be back, Mr Molloy. I am sure of it.

I can walk away from you any time, Miss Laskowski. And I will. Right this minute.

No, Mr Molloy. I don't think so.

25

Miguelito wraps Jackie Molloy in the finest silk and muslin and bears him aloft beyond violence, to have and to hold unto death, on the journey to the dark interior.

Sweat pours off in the scorching heat. Miguelito bathes Jackie's brow in frankincense and myrrh, restoration of a skin to shelter nerves, veins, and blood. Cannot lay bare the circuitry and reduce to black cinder paths, Miguelito's arms then to become a bier, until until—

The courage. Having lacked, do not wait again. This second chance, this last. Return in time, see in time, get to the Valentine before the future descends and daylight goes out for ever.

Cannot.

Must.

Will.

No, Molloy. Lie back. You going to wear you self out. You been making sounds like a jungle, you in a forest someplace and I'm telling you, you got things coming at you from trees and shadows, oh man when that happen you got to rest, you got to go someplace safe. Lie back.

Georgie, Georgie, you can't find me
  Oh yeah I can, I'll find you
  I hiding

One two three ready or not here I come

Not yet, Georgie, it's too quick

Hey come on, that's the game ain't it, hide-and-seek, and I say ready-or-not and you gotta be ready or I win, so I win

But I not ready, Georgie, go again

You come out from under that table, Jackie Molloy, it's a stupid goddamn game

No, Georgie, you have to play right

Whaddya mean right, what the hell is wrong with how I play, you givin' me lip? Get out from under there, you're lucky I even play your lousy games, you think I got nothin' better to do than play stupid games with a fuckin' baby, get up here

No, it's not fair

I'm the one says what's fair, I'm the mother, Jackie Molloy, so you got three seconds to get up here and you know what happens after three seconds

No, Georgie! Don't count three!

One

I sorry, I sorry, here I come!

Two

Stop!

Three. All right get up here you little piece of shit, there now, I smacked you because you gave me lip and I'm the grown-up, what does that fucking father of yours think I am, a babysitter? Huh? A maid? Him and his big important meetings, here's one for him, too, leaving me all by myself, what kind of a boyfriend is he, he don't even bring me out, and you cut out that cryin', that wasn't even a hard slap, you'll see a hard slap if you keep this up, now sit over there, I'll get you a Coke and we'll play cards, good boy, that's it, fold your hands nice in front of you. You want ice?

No thank you

Good boy, now, we'll have our drinks, I want ice, just a

little vodka in there first, then a little Coke, why, we're great old pals aren't we Jackie Molloy, you and me, I'm only tryin' to teach you things, never mind about Mick, who needs him anyway, hey, you want to know something really secret, lean over here to me, doll, I got to whisper, there's always some jerk listening behind these walls, big ears all of them, closer, come on, okay: you know why your father's in all those meetings?

No

He's in those meetings 'cause there's going to be a big strike! You know what a strike is? Well I'll tell you what a strike is, it's gonna be where Mick and all the other men won't work any more 'til the owners start treatin' them right, you get it? Good boy, and your Daddy is in charge of it, see? We're so proud of him, aren't we, he's the one organising the men, then after the strike we'll have more money and we'll get a house, that's what a strike is, so now drink your Coke and we'll play Go Fish, I'll just get myself a little refill, you deal them out, honey

Get in the fuckin' door, you'll do what I say

I don't wanna, Mick, why do you make me, why do you

'Cause we got no money, that's why, how can I marry you and get you a house if we got no money, wake up the kid and be quiet, place is crawlin' with scabs and spies and every other type of low life, I'm gonna move us out of here anyway

I don't wanna move yet, Mick, we moved three times this month already

Shut up, where's the kid, he's not in the bed, what did I tell you about watchin' him

How could I watch him if I was out with you, how could—

What the hell is this?

Oh yeah he puts the blanket over the table and sleeps under there

You let him do that? I told you, tuck him in at night, what do you call this?

I'll get him Mick, let me, don't worry, it's just a game

Hey! Wake up! We got visitors coming

Come on honey that's it, your Georgie's here, you're all sleepy aren't you, fell asleep in your little tent

Wash him, give him a fresh T-shirt

For Christ sake, Mick, it's three o'clock in the morning

Did you hear what I told you?

Mick! Don't, don't! Aw, Mick, that hurt

Get over there, Jackie, Georgie's gonna dress you up for the company and there's more where that came from if you don't shut your mouth, you want a nice house? A car?

You know I do Mick, I love you baby, that's all that counts

Then there's certain things you gotta do, I'm doin' my bit, I can't do any more, I'm at it day and night, I'm a marked man, Georgie, none of them will give me work, not 'til it's over, not 'til we win, then they'll remember Mick Molloy, then we'll have dollar bills to burn, but right now I need you, come here to me

Nobody kisses like you Mick

You have me first Georgie, just think of me and you'll be fine, that's it, that's how you like it Mick knows how

Mick, oh

Come on baby come on

Oh yeah Mick yeah

There you go there you go

Mick Mick

That's it baby that's what you'll remember tonight, hey you like that Jackie? You like to see that?

'Course he likes that, don't you Jackie, see how happy Georgie is – Jesus Mick they're here!

Hold on, fellas, hold on! Give me a minute! Keep your voices down! Straighten up the bed Georgie, put Jackie on the chair, you behave yourself Jackie, these are important men, they're your friends

I'm ready Mick I'm with you all the way

Hey now all of you, get in here, for Christ sake a bunch of drunks, you'll have every fuckin' shipowner woke up, Gene how are ya, Joe, Harry, drinks for everybody, Georgie, you all know Georgie, Pete good man you brought Bill, yeah, hi Bill, hey this here's my boy Jackie, that's it, shake their hands, come on, stand up and say hello

Oh Christ he's got a good grip on him Mick

Damn right, where's those drinks Georgie

Let's see you flex them muscles for old Bill, aren't you a big fella

You heard him Jackie, go on

Oh now I'm telling you, we're signin' you up Jackie Molloy, look at him, he's strong, Mick, I mean it

Of course, what else would he be, drink up boys and then Georgie here will give you a little fun after a hard day, you can count on Mick

Here's to you and the ILA, Mick

International Longshoremen's Association, hip-hip, hooray!

Here's to you, Georgie, good woman!

Hey Georgie give us a little peek

I'm first

Go on get up on the table there, let's see what you got

Hey Pete she don't do nothin' 'til I see the greenbacks, hundred apiece, as many times as you can get it up and in

Hundred! Hey!

You heard me, take it or leave it, you still got work, they won't touch me – okay, that's it, hand it right here to old Mick, let me just count it, yeah, five hundred dollars, okay Georgie, so what do you want her to do first

A little dance
Yeah!
Yeah! Let's get a good look at ya
Okay fellas you asked for it, here I go
Kiss me Georgie
How's that Bill, you like that? Come on, the rest of you, don't be shy, come here for a little kiss, fix me another drink, Mick
Hey look what I got for you Georgie, grab it, oh boy
On the table, let's see ya do it
Hey I was first

Don't go with them, Mick, stay with me, Mick! What'd I do wrong? I did what you said, I did everything.

Mick!

You fuckin' bastard! Ten dollars! You throw ten dollars at me after what I did for you, come back here, I want my share, you're nothin' without me, you and your stupid union, nothin'!

Thanks Jackie the hell with him anyway, who needs him, help me up, good boy, sleep, we gotta sleep, just pour me one more drink, honey, then we'll lie down, a little drink and you'll come and lie down with your Georgie, that's it, oh the bed feels good don't it, there, you have some, too, help you sleep, take a sip, yeah, then come lie right here, right in close, you're cold aren't you, that's it, you feel them all you want, get nice and warm, you need to sleep

26

If only the elements would stay where they belong, sequence of events/time factor/all. Jackie *was* twenty-five, *is* sixty. Was sixty, is twenty-five. Girl is dead, girl alive, Anna knows Marilyn, Marilyn knows Anna, the girl the girl the girl. Dead alive dead alive, Chuck is here and there and gone, and Bobby sees Jackie sees Bobby. Which is then and which is now and what will be?

Get back to Levittown, explain to Bobby.

I told you, Molloy, you cannot go no place. You got a fever.

Thirsty.

Miguelito raises Jackie's head and puts a Chinese teacup to his lips. Schizandra, jasmine paniculatum, ginseng, and limeflower blend with the juices of grapes, elderflowers, and elderberries in cool sparkling water. Jackie's burnt and burning parchment throat, cracked and split in the long drought, jumps as Miguelito's balm spreads.

Miguelito lowers Jackie's head, places a cool cloth on his brow. He irrigates the arms again, first with warm water, then oils. A supple blend of lavender, rosewood, and neroli.

Better. Better.

Now you ready to go to you Levittown place, Jackie. Go where you need to go, see what you need to see. But you not getting up from this table or travelling out of my sights. Pretty soon night will come down, the day be over. Then maybe you are alive again.

Miguelito places Jackie's sunglasses carefully over his eyes. Behind the darkness, through the camouflage, creatures of the night work their way.

Why why why?

Such an elusive, that Jackie should return so soon again to the bush across from 143.

That there should be no lights at the Wilmots', no life on the street. Whose houses this night trail each other as if a cortège.

Why does Jackie believe a clue will appear in the window of a bungalow on Long Island?

Whatever would give rise to a flame flickering code across verges from a window such as this? When saints and temples in far-off holy places have failed to shed light?

A Valentine, a leather wreath laid on a restaurant table. What is the sense of roses-are-red abandoned in a callbox? Of the circumference of a belt?

Tomorrow Jackie will cancel Washington. Marty will gloat about how he persuaded him to stay, too bad pal, I know him a long time, I knew he'd come around, and then he'll let Jackie do anything he wants.

Straining, seeking, the binoculars reveal nothing. Or is empty space a clue? Absence presence?

Presence.

Jackie freezes.

Another child is playing in the floating light. This is what happens in Levittown. For these young there are no ghosts behind the billowing hovering cloak of nightfall that sweeps them lacking fear into play and darkness. Of course: any child could be on the playground, that is the way of safe places, to be inhabited. The cortège is the procession of events and times in Jackie Molloy, not in this community.

But the new child is not concentrating.

Bounce, bounce.

Stop.

Not really interested.

Wait a minute: leather-soled shoes. Not a child. Did Bobby tell someone? Has someone been waiting?

Sound ceases. No ball, no feet.

The arid claws of dread reach for Jackie Molloy, the playground now too still. Not right, no tap-tap. Silence beyond silence, void beyond the void, Georgie Georgie

He wants to scream.

Slowly, inexorably, a pair of hands opens the crypt. Parts the tangled branches exactly where they wait to be parted.

Jackie cowers against the far edge of his tomb as another form crawls in, turns on a small electric lantern, and illuminates.

Bobby, Bobby, past and present. He is wearing his suit and tie and best shoes. On his knees he studies Jackie Molloy across the canyon left between the times.

Jackie shields his face against light that is now upon his degradation, do not see, do not look, do not know, you are a child.

Get out, leave me alone!

I won't hurt you, mister.

Jackie raises his face. A man's clothes and infant's skin. Jackie's eyes meet the rift in the sickening light.

He lunges, pushing and kicking at the unwelcome boy, Go away, go away, as Bobby Wilmot tumbles back out of the hideaway and disappears.

27

In his room, on his bed, on his back, 1959. Later.

Jackie Molloy is trying, all his fading feeble might, hollowed-out rind, to fend off the clutch of a wide-eyed boy and the gasp from a sinking callbox.

Why why and how, Anna, Marilyn, and the girl? And that child. What should bring him back and back to Jackie, what does a boy of all creations have to do with any of this?

Swimming and perhaps drowning.

Quick: bunch up in a ball. Roll, kick. Lash the arms through tentacles crawling toward the neck. Lean down to the floor, put the head hard against the floor, again again, knock the chains off. Arrest the muffled gurgling of the callbox as tide and current draw the coffin of violets-are-blue into the deep.

There: freedom.

Make for the surface.

But up there is light, sound, air.

Quick again, oh the shortage of time.

Jam anything against any opening. Plug the ears, nose, mouth, eyes, and anus with sand, close off entrances.

Jackie bounds from the bed to the sink to the drawers in search of stoppers, and in the bathroom down the hall savages the earth from a dead plant, ramming it into the holes, the chinks in the armour required above water.

He staggers back to his room dripping crumbs, forehead black and blue, and lies on the bed tasting his grave.

Then something comes to him in the blackout.

Urge.

Fans out across his skin and itching clogged eyes like fresh linen. Thank God not to *see* what arrives and demands entry. But I forgot about skin. Forgot about *feel.*

Desire.

He holds the sides of the bed, stiffens himself into a seizure and slaps the bed like a plank, Grand Mal Grand Mal, discharge, release, disperse, shake off sensation, be a piece of wood, convey nothing.

He is spent.

But the drive is not dead or even tamed. Only tired.

And now Jackie knows, oh how cruel it is to know.

He wants this girl.

This incarnation. This intimately recognised.

Who is she? Why has she come? What gives an avatar power over skin?

And what can it mean, to want? One manifestation in a body meeting another? This is not the wanting of Mulligans, Franks and Joannes. The come-and-go of do-it-and-pay. No, this is the wanting that pulls skin apart like threads of cloth, and transforms it into a hatched wrapping that reveals organs. And allows dark viscous urgencies from the girl to pass through by osmosis. Until finally the substances saturate, and cannot be withdrawn without convulsion and hallucination. Oh this craving, this necessity, this *must drink, must soak in*. No, absorption is not the wanting of Mulligans, Franks and Joannes.

Jackie turns and lies on his stomach, oh that is a bad bump, Georgie will make it better, you didn't know I could sing, did you, now listen I'll make it into a song: Jackie and Jill went up the hill to fetch a pail of water – See? Everything was going fine for them, just like you, you were all happy today, and then, Jackie fell down and broke his crown – well, you don't have a crown, but anyway – and Jill came tumbling after, so things worked out! And that's a story about a fall, Jackie Molloy, like you had today, Jackie Molloy aged thirteen had a fall and a bad bump. Show me where it hurts, oh yeah, right there on your back, I can see, it's all red. Here's a new crown for you, hey a pie plate looks good on you. Just lie there, I'm gonna rub in a little Vaseline, make your skin feel all better, and then we'll have a drink to warm us up.

Georgie undresses the boy who lies in a feigned sleep in the dingy room allowing the woman's hands to move over his back, at once carefully seeking the hurt and roughing him up as she yanks clothing over his head and down his legs. Jackie is young adult thirteen, and the meaning of to want is in this, however approximate, however come-and-go, this and this alone, to want.

Now Georgie's clothes. Jackie places his left cheek against the grimy sheet and sees her bra and her panties on the chair. Her blouse and skirt. His heart skips. The bed will rock. This is their game.

Does she know it is a game, this business of I-have-hurt-my-back-Georgie? Between his legs he is expanding. He aches. Soon his groin will want to explode. He closes his eyes.

Their unspoken ritual: now Georgie is at the fridge getting ice. She is humming. She too is filled with anticipation, the splendour of the time in awaiting, oh the clink of that ice in the glass, chimes, bells, and the top taken off the gin bottle, how to describe the sound of that top spinning off and into Georgie's hand, the dance of that top, the splash of the gin over the ice, the way Georgie swishes the two together letting them play, and then her first sip, Ah Jackie now that's what I call a refreshing drink. And always always the same way, she comes to the side of the bed and kneels, and concealing her breasts she says, Open your eyes for a sec, a little drink of this will help that bruise on your back, and she tips the glass sideways towards Jackie's mouth and some of the gin goes in, some trickles down his chin and on to the sheet and Georgie runs her tongue across Jackie's mouth. His eyes close again, Georgie gets up. A warm stream ambles through Jackie, he is being bathed in a spa, he is awash with soothing tingling waters and the pounding in his groin begins. His legs are rubber, he now knows every inch of his body, all outposts are in a state of high alert, excitement, ringing alarms, as he listens to Georgie padding about the room in her bare feet and still the humming. The glass is refilled. The ritual is about to progress.

Georgie turns off the light. Balmy glow from the street like the touch of her hands. She approaches the bed. She unscrews the lid of the Vaseline and drops this to the floor. Her excitement is building, too, she cannot be bothered with the lid, and as always Jackie pretends to sleep. There we are, all relaxed, my poor Jackie had a bad fall today, you just sleep, that's it. Georgie dips into the Vaseline, rubs it on to her hands, we'll make that sore back all better, and the hands glide across the boy's buttocks, sending sparks down his legs, hands pull and push and grab the buttocks, draw designs in the Vaseline and move like silk down over the boy's hips, lift him gently and massage between his legs, soft and then harder, and Georgie begins to groan. Jackie is throbbing, can hardly contain, but the wait, the waiting, this is to want, and Georgie too will try to hold back as long as she can, she reaches down for the glass of gin sitting on the floor, gulps it, can no longer speak, she now kneels over Jackie, pushes her hands up Jackie's back, leans on his back, digs for more Vaseline and greases the boy up and down, electrifying him, hardening him, and in a moment he will lift himself and unbeknownst to Georgie in her ecstasy he will tuck his hands under his abdomen where they will move slowly down between his legs and begin to grind, do it now: Georgie has placed the Vaseline back on the floor, she is about to mount again. Jackie's hands cup his swollen genitals, he is floating on a magic carpet, he is outside and above the boundaries of tenement walls, as Georgie throws one leg and then the other over Jackie's body. Straddling him on her knees she presses herself against him and groans. Jackie can feel her arch her back as she parts his buttocks and grinds her thick mound into him, he can feel the abundant wet tangle as she twists and thrusts, pressing Jackie's hands harder and harder against himself, he is hot and thundering but he can still wait, Georgie is not ready, he can feel she wants more waiting, more holding off, make the floating last, and now, in the next step, Georgie leans forward, stretches out across Jackie's back, and gyrates her breasts the length of his body, splays one breast and then the other against his buttocks, heaps of soft flesh and jelly smoothing soothing, and Jackie's hands now massage quickly as Georgie mounts again, moans again, pushes Jackie's back, and pumps herself faster and faster. He grabs and pulls himself in perfect harmony with her thrusts, and then—

Oh God then—

Jackie Molloy 1959 hurls himself from the bed, not let this continue, not let the next part, his head under the roaring tap, cold cold over this hot seeping memory, and Jackie's scalp is frozen, a cap of ice over a path to remembrance, blocking it at the moment just before—

1994 Jackie leaps from Miguelito's table, Third Avenue Third Avenue, back to Third Avenue, time is running out, and against his friend's pleading, bolts out of the shop, away from the closing in.

Jackie Molloy, unbandaged wounds exposed to air and

light, looks for another place to hide and discovers a dank alley with vermin. He climbs into a skip and nestles with the garbage, thirty-five years to the day, where merciful unconsciousness again overtakes.

28

But does not spare him the return.

1959: yes, his skull is anaesthetised for the moment against recall of Georgie. Yet, on his bed again, he discovers that he has not managed to quench the Valentine, or the meeting of the girl with Marilyn and Anna. Bobby is quiet, resting somewhere in far reaches, as if he had never happened.

Jackie now begins, logically, to lay out the pieces of the jigsaw in the air before his wide open eyes, in a skip in a dream of days past. In delicate movements of vision he can move pieces nearer together to try a fit, or further apart when he sees no connection. A search for the centre, a search for the margins.

The girl knew I was following her. Has known all along. She purchased the Valentine on her way to a meeting with people she knows and should not know. No doubt realising that I am aware of the anomaly, she wanted to tell me something, explain something about that meeting, her relationship to Marilyn and Anna. She may even have wanted me to witness it. Overhear. I hesitated, went back too late for the card, and she thought I wasn't coming. But then I arrived without knowing I had arrived. She, of course, thought I had arrived intentionally, based on her plea in the Valentine. That is, if she even saw me in the coffee shop. Which certainly she did. She has seen me everywhere, she knows I am near. There must be a connection between the Valentine and the meeting. Yes.

And me.

Me.

What do I have to do with it?

She needs me.

For what?

Help.

She wants help.

What most people want.

One person approximate to another will ask above all: help me.

And, same breath, especially nearing the last, that person will also say: Please.

Please help me. Help me please.

Help with what?

Oh, God: and did the Valentine say *how*? How to help? Or *when*?

Jackie wants to rocket from his room and go after the girl and ask all the questions.

But if I had been paying attention I would already know the answers, the answers were in the Valentine. If she had wanted to speak otherwise to me, speak aloud in words, words that are lost to the air upon contact, she would not have written the card, wherein words can be kept and held and remembered when contact is gone.

He must respect her decision, she must know best, must know the need for her words not to disappear into air but to be written down for all time. These are not his boundaries to violate, the situation must be serious. And secret. And whatever she said must have been very clear.

Why why did he forsake the Valentine?

Never mind. No time now for recrimination.

Time now for putting pieces together. Logic.

Clues.

Everyone is at the table.

Except.

Chuck.

Everyone at the table knows Chuck.

Everyone at the table knows what Chuck is doing.

Betraying.

Never mind how they all got together. It doesn't matter. Well, it might matter, but it can't matter now, only the consequences matter now, what consequence their meeting.

Yes: I am to help with the consequence. Outcome. That's it.

So the question is: what came of that meeting? Something was decided, or confirmed, and that is why the girl asks my help now and not earlier. *Now* it has been decided.

It.

What?

People get together, include some, exclude others.

Why exclude Chuck?

Ah: to talk about Chuck. Always the someone left out is the someone talked about.

Chuck the betrayer.

Betrayer of his wife and family.

Perhaps betrayer of the girl because he will not leave the wife and family.

And Anna? How has he betrayed Anna? What does the girl have to do with Anna?

Can't know for sure, but assume a betrayal of Anna, too.

Assume that betrayal by Chuck brings these three together. Therefore Chuck is eliminated. Four minus one, he is the betrayer, they went to the coffee shop to talk about Chuck.

Careful, Jackie, careful.

What did you just say?

Scramble off the bed to his locker, files from work, where is my dictionary, here it is, eliminate eliminate: to remove or take out; to reject; omit from consideration; slang: *to murder in cold blood.*

The belt.

The belt.

Oh Jackie you do not need a dictionary to know what you have just said and what they were doing in that coffee shop, to know the logic of the puzzle as it now fits together in the air before your eyes.

Chuck is to be strangled with the belt. By the three women he has betrayed.

Think, Jackie: what help would the girl need from you?

You have these two pieces, a call for help and a plan to murder Chuck. Now put them together.

Perhaps the three women have not decided who will do the actual killing. Or maybe Anna and Marilyn have demanded the girl be the one. She the one to be sacrificed to the police, a decoy away from Anna and Marilyn, the one with the least to lose. This is perhaps the reparation she must make, the price of infidelity, she is, after all, the source of the betrayal, the temptress, and so she will now be asked to put her love to death and then stand trial and be executed herself.

Justice: the girl siphons off guilt and shame, cleansing and purifying Anna and Marilyn.

So the girl is a betrayer, too. She and Chuck together. Anna and Marilyn are the betrayed. That's it.

Jackie paces.

The girl is to be Chuck's killer. The others will force her to kill the man she loves by imposing a choice: either they murder him, or she does. If the girl refuses the task, the other two women will vow to carry it out in a prolonged and brutal manner. If, on the other hand, the girl agrees to kill Chuck herself, they will provide her with gentler means, drugs or poison, that will spare Chuck any pain or foreknowledge of his own death. She won't warn him, or go to the police. Her betrayal of the secret of their relationship to Anna and Marilyn would be revealed. Besides, she probably feels certain there will be a way out: me. What the girl does not know, of course, is that either way, Anna and Marilyn will build the case against her and betray her to the police, and in the end she will no doubt be tried and executed for the crime. The two traitors will have paid the price.

So is she asking that I help her kill Chuck? Or is she asking that I help her get away afterward? Help her thwart the second part of Anna and Marilyn's plan?

Jackie turns this dilemma over and over like a prism.

But light keeps dispersing, refusing to converge on one point, breaking up in all directions.

Jackie sighs. He let the Valentine get away.

He must now wait for another instruction and hope he understands its meaning.

29

Jackie Molloy pulls himself up to the edge of the rancid skip. As he shifts, a rat pushes its way up through the garbage and scrambles away from the interloper.

He swings one leg and then the other over the side and jumps to the ground. Picks scraps off his clothes and carefully extracts bits of mouldy food from the tears on his arms. Did he just have a dream? Or is it in the reality in the present day of all days that logic has come back to him? Come back in order to be defied?

For at this moment Jackie believes in his heart of hearts that he will not allow events in the second chance to progress in the manner of the first. Oh no, this time he will arrive well in advance. He will have retrieved the Valentine and followed instructions.

Must clean myself up, a job to do, tell Marty I won't be in for a while, very big job.

Jackie's head is an empty shell. He has not eaten for almost two days, his body is depleted and shaking, he is dizzy, swirling.

But his mind races like a train, click-clack click-clack, everything on edge, sharp. Switches flip and trains divert, tracks meet and part, sudden thoughts take off, leave tracks and move with the alacrity of jets and just as suddenly land. The brakes scream, pushed to the utmost, thoughts rush back to the station, aloft to grounded, air to earth and back again, as atoms gather speed faster faster faster just before the collision, split seconds, crucial seconds.

Back to the apartment, clean myself up.

Get to the No Name.

Jackie washes himself in the sink. Ice water. He moves like a machine. Stiff, jerky arms and hands fold the towel perfectly, lay it perfectly. There. Now. Okay.

Jackie is tiptoeing on a fine line between his alertness – sounds and lights and colours, twitches and starts of awareness, the brain starved and strung out, feeding on its own impulses – and a mind about to snap. A mind pulled as tight as elastic, giving off a high-pitched whine as it stretches further and further toward the limits of design and intention.

Slow down, slow down, a lot to do. Think.

The No Name.

Third Avenue.

Long-sleeve shirt over the wounds, no bandages, they'll be fine, Miguelito said 'air'. Khakis, sneakers.

Jackie pushes his taut springy strands of legs through a barrier. Body split off from mind, both split off from susceptibility.

Chop-chop, left-right, go-stop, unimpeded through crowds, Ah! Marty! Almost forgot! Three blocks to the *Mirror* building.

Through the massive doors, recognise them anywhere, and into the lift.

Fourth floor, please. *Mirror* Editorial. I guess Tommy's off today.

Who?

Did you hear what I said? *Mirror* Editorial.

Mirror? Hey—

Fourth floor! Who's your supervisor?

There ain't no supervisor, asshole, and this ain't no *Mirror* building. The *Mirror* went out of business in 1968. You're a little late.

Open these doors.

Pleasure. Go fuck yourself.

Never mind, for Christ sake I know this is today, I didn't really think I could go back, just wanted to take a look. I know what I'm doing.

Third Avenue. South-east corner of 63rd and Third.

1994: Tower Records.

10 March 1959: No Name Bar.

Now that Jackie has figured out what will happen – Chuck will be murdered and the girl accused – he is confident. He needs only to watch for another signal: what help and when. In the meantime he will remain close. He will let her know that he knows. He will be present to her as long as she requires.

Since Valentine's Day he has followed Chuck and the girl without subterfuge or disguise. They have seemed quiet and contented.

There is an eerie stillness in the configurations of this story, an absence of urgency. Is this feeling only in Jackie's imagination?

Or could it be that he is not the only one waiting?

Not the only one suspended in the time between the lighting of the fuse and the detonation of the bomb? Contemplating the long slow snake sizzling and rattling to its predestined end, the strike?

At the same time, Chuck and the girl haven't met as frequently as usual. A sign, perhaps, of her withdrawal. Chuck will soon be dead.

But Jackie recalls two particular meetings: one outside Chuck's office, where the girl waited for her lover at five. And one on the Third Avenue bus, again. Both these times Jackie stood boldly near the couple, and both times the girl acknowledged him.

The look in her eyes was new: a light had come. The droop seemed less pronounced. Yes: she is relieved. She is grateful. She knows I will protect her. She was looking for a way out and she found me. This is what her eyes are saying.

In the security of the girl's recognition Jackie no longer obsesses about her. He is no longer driven to follow her. Something tells him all is well for the moment, she just needs to know he knows. He stops meeting Frank and Joanne, Marty makes him his second-in-command as the reward for giving up Washington, and he works with unbounded energy and interest.

The night of 10 March 1959, in front of the No Name, Jackie Molloy is an assured man.

Although something he cannot define has brought him here, where he has not been in weeks, on this night.

He watches Chuck and the girl approach. As casually as if they had agreed to meet.

Jackie can tell that she does not yet see him. He studies them unashamedly. Chuck is far too rigid for her. Too proper. She is holding his arm loosely. She is relaxed, he is tense. She is wearing flat shoes in which she nearly shuffles. She is self-conscious. She is worried about the fact that she exists.

Chuck has never lost the military bearing. His walk is formal and correct, the feet move like cogs in a wheel, each step locked in place. He is a pseudo-man, thinks Jackie.

I would be better for her.

He blushes.

And then he is horrified.

For he suddenly realises that he, too, would like Charles J. Wilmot III to die.

He panics. He cannot allow the girl to witness his depravity, she is bound to sense it. She will hate him for this wish to destroy the man she loves, how could anyone accept such a base motive for offering help.

So he turns away and tucks himself into a throng of shoppers before she sees his humiliation, the sinister glee covering his face like a birthmark.

The street is crowded. Chuck and the girl slip into the bar unnoticed. Jackie has managed to remain hidden.

Now he has a dilemma. Will he follow them in?

Why?

Is it really necessary to let the girl know he is near?

She seems fine, probably doesn't need him tonight.

Strange: I've never wanted to avoid her before.

Her?

I can hardly bear to be away.

No.

And then Jackie realises: it is Chuck he does not want to see. He cannot stand him. And he is afraid Chuck will discover him and retaliate.

He paces quickly, up-down, up-down, trying to shake off. Wants to take a knife to this brain of his, cut out the offending thoughts, the shocking thoughts, and he imagines a knife, slice slice, the bad parts of the meat excised, the blood wiped, the scars gone, no trace.

Stick to the goal, you are getting away from the goal.

The goal is to guard this girl. That is what she is asking of you. All else is immaterial. It is imperative that she continue to see you watching. Waiting patiently and attentively for her instructions.

He enters the No Name. Again and again he has made this descent.

But somehow tonight there seem to be more stairs than usual and he feels himself going further down.

Chuck and the girl are at the far table where he saw her once by herself. A time that now seems years, and Jackie wishes.

He places himself well inside the door, fully visible, and stares openly at his two subjects. Their heads are inclined toward each other. They are speaking confidences. Intimacies. See? I can stand and watch them. Doesn't affect me.

Don't lie, Jackie: you have just felt a rush. The rush of murder. Chuck's murder. You have just imagined doing it yourself.

Ah, but this is why I feel no jealousy. Chuck is going to die. The reality is that he will not last. I am the one who will last. Besides, he thinks she is sharing everything with him. But she isn't: he doesn't know about me. That is *our* secret.

Jackie is gripped by these murderous hateful longings, no wonder the stairwell seems to go down and down, his heart is pounding with the pleasures of pornographic imaginings, mutilations of this arrogant half-man who has placed the woman he claims to love in the path of destruction, who will now get the ultimate answer himself for his neglect and incompetence, oh he'll see how far his stupidity got him.

Stop, Jackie, stop, somehow.

The girl needs your understanding. When this is over, when she has succeeded in killing Chuck, she will need comfort. She does not *want* to lose him, no. This is not her choice, to murder her lover, she is being forced and she will need your protection above all, she will need from you only the purest thoughts and clearest actions.

Quick to the bar: a double Scotch.

In the mirror behind the bar his eyes are wild. As he has never before seen them.

Get a hold. Deep breath.

Act casual.

He turns. Stares again.

Why doesn't she look up at me?

To the left of the table is a callbox. Chuck holds her hand. She is very unhappy.

She takes her hand away from him and fumbles in her purse. He produces change and she rises reluctantly from the table. She is going to make a phone call.

Maybe she is trying to reach me! Maybe she decided to tell Chuck about the plan to kill him, she can't go through with it, and now wants me to help them both escape. Jackie feels his insides begin to liquify as hope departs.

For God's sake, she doesn't even know my name! Don't be ridiculous!

Who is she calling?

Jackie gulps another double and while the girl's back is to him he takes a seat at the table next to hers. Chuck is nursing what looks like straight bourbon. He winces with every sip. Not ginger ale. But necessary.

The girl has dialled a number. She is waiting for a reply, leaning over the callbox.

Jackie feels he must overhear this call, for he has decided, during the second drink, that she is going to kill Chuck tonight, she cannot wait, and this is the reason for her unhappiness. She has given him some excuse for her mood, an excuse perhaps connected to this phone call.

Could today's date and time and place have been contained in the Valentine? Perhaps this is exactly where Jackie is meant to be at this moment.

He is about to explode. He clenches his fists for control. He vows that if the murder does *not* occur tonight, he will never again, from this minute forward, let the girl out of his sight. He will not repeat the agony of missing another call for help.

Someone has answered on the other end.

Jackie cannot make out what the girl is saying. He strains. He is hearing the words, most of them. But does not understand them. Why not? Perhaps she is still speaking too softly, yes, that is true, he is unable to catch every word.

Jackie yearns for another drink. But cannot dare to leave

his post. The girl's voice is rising to a furious whisper and at last Jackie hears clearly.

She is not speaking English.

Not speaking English?

Impossible. Listen again, Jackie.

Jackie is bowled over. The girl hangs up. He has not held on to one word or one sound of the language he has just heard.

Ah! Wait a minute! That is exactly the point. To exclude the listener. Chuck excluded again. Chuck is being deceived. He has not, after all, been let in on the plan. He is still being kept out.

Jackie watches Chuck again, Chuck struggling to tolerate bourbon. If he could, Jackie would laugh out loud at him and his impotence, he's too limp even for a stiff drink, how do you get stiffer than a bourbon, and there sits Charles J. Wilmot III, soft and mushy, the only thing hard about him is the glass of bourbon in his flaccid hand.

The girl is back at the table.

Jackie looks right at her.

The startle shows fleetingly around the eyes which are instantly covered with a mask that shows only a flicker of recognition. Otherwise her eyes are—

Oh, God, Jackie, you don't want to see that again, you thought that was over. The chill in her eyes.

Why would she have that look just now? And for you?

She must be steeling herself for what she is about to do.

Of course.

She cannot weaken now. She cannot let on to Chuck that she knows a man at another table. How would she explain that? I have never come this close to her – maybe I've overstepped.

That's it: she's nervous. Pull back.

Jackie picks up his glass, returns to the bar for another

double. The alcohol is barely reaching him. Every inch of his body is wired.

He turns to face the girl again.

Ah, now: a slight smile in Jackie's direction. Jackie smiles back. Chuck is hunched over the drink he can't drink, the manhood to which he cannot rise, oblivious. How can he be so stupid? He is assisting at his own death.

The girl looks away from Jackie and takes Chuck's hand. Only a few sips of the elixir and he is getting drunk. She helps him up and they begin to walk toward the door to leave.

Wait a minute: why aren't they going upstairs?

Jackie freezes. Is there a change of plan? He realises he has assumed she would kill him upstairs, where no one would find the body for days.

But what do you mean, Jackie, 'change?'. You don't even *know* the plan. How will you know if it changes?

He scrambles to pay the bartender. As the girl exits after Chuck, she turns back to Jackie, and through the small window of the weathered door he sees that the eyes are starved, pleading to be fed the light. They are shrunk into dark hollows, seeming almost to be sucked into the infinity of her skull, and the lips, too, are defeated, it is a heavy sorrow pulling down the lips, she can barely survive the struggle, she is being drawn in and in and down. And then she goes.

Jackie is desperate. He rushes out of the No Name and on to Third Avenue. Has he missed yet another instruction?

Chuck and the girl proceed west to Lexington Avenue and walk down Lexington to the girl's apartment building.

Jackie wants to shout, his fists clench and unclench like the disembodied twisted knot his heart has become, and the bones in his chest feel ready to snap. Have mercy, have mercy, give me another clue, I am here, I am here, tell me what to do.

Chuck and the girl pause outside her building.

She gropes in her handbag for keys. Fumbles, drops the bag by a bush at the entrance, and the contents spill out.

She and Chuck are stunned. They stand immobilised over the dashed container, all the private and personal seepage strewn at their feet, precious belongings lost hold of.

They bend down in a confused and harried state, to try and put right.

But the day is disappearing into darkness. An ominous night is coming down upon the lost and broken pieces dropped from the safety of the little bag. There is no way Chuck and the girl can put them back the way they were.

They rise and slump together, clutching the bruised satchel between them like beggars.

It is over, thinks Jackie Molloy. Nothing is said, but they both know it. I am the witness.

He waits outside the apartment building for the girl to emerge after the killing. Ready to comfort her, take her away.

But, no. No. Why bother ever again with hope?

At four a.m. Chuck comes through the doors. Jacket and tie flung over his shoulder. He is whistling.

Jackie is numb. Exhausted. Wound up to a high and smashed to the ground.

Chuck and the girl have had a night of sex.

Go, Jackie. Go from these torments.

But release is not the case for Jackie Molloy. Severed scattered parts return.

He sees beside the bush at the building's entrance a white ball of paper. And then he knows: the real reason for the spillage. Not keys.

His heart leaps. He reaches. He holds.

Lightness of paper, sawdust in time to come.

Jackie with reverence opens the fragile treasure.

The precious clue, at last.

And reads.

Please

30

Uh, right. Mom, Dad, this is the reporter I was telling you about, he's covering the story – thanks – yeah – just put it over there, I'll sort it out later. Did you get the stain out of the white shirt?

What for? I threw it out.

You threw it out? Mom, for God's sake! What did—

You don't have a job, Chuckie. You got fired.

I still like to wear a white shirt once in a while, Mom, it doesn't matter if I don't go to an office, I—

It might not matter to *you*, but it does matter to *some* people. Doesn't it, Father?

You've ruined our lives, son. I'm sorry to say it, but it's true.

Oh, Jesus, never mind, drop it. All because of a white shirt. Look, the point is to meet this reporter, Mr Molloy. He's trying to find the murderer, he's doing his best to clear my name.

I am?

Well, I guess that's not the exact thing, not exactly, I mean, I don't mean *literally*, just overall. Like in a friendly way you'll hopefully put the best slant on the situation.

You mean *lie*, Chuckie? You are asking this nice man to lie for you?

No, not *lie*, Mom, he won't need to. As he gets to know

me, know my background, he'll realise I couldn't have done it.

What an asshole you are, Wilmot. You think I give a shit who did it? Sins of commission and all that? What about *omission*?

I don't think we need to use language like *that*, Mr – what was his name again, Chuckie?

Molloy. And you cut it out, Molloy, or you're leaving.

Uh, son, is he all right?

There's nothing the matter with him, Dad.

He just fell asleep.

Yeah, I mean, I guess he's tired, that's all.

Chuckie, he's been drinking. You've both been drinking.

Mom, come on. Quit imagining things.

I can smell it. Don't lie. One lie after another. I didn't bring you up that way.

It must be something else you smell.

I bought you that wine, I know how it smells. He didn't even say 'Nice to meet you.'

Look, he covers a lot of stories, this is only one assignment, he's under pressure all the time. He didn't mean not to say he's pleased to meet you. Jesus. Molloy! Wake up!

I heard her, I heard her. Yeah. Nice to meet you both. Sorry – rough night. Deadlines. Wasn't thinking straight when you came in. But actually I do want to talk to you. Your son is such a lovely person.

Cut the crap, Molloy.

Mr Molloy, my wife and I just want you to know he did not learn those words at home.

I'm sure he didn't, Mr Wilmot, he just got in with a very bad element after he moved out.

That's just about enough, Molloy!

Chuckie, be still for a few moments while Mr Molloy interviews us. Now. What should I tell you about? And will my name go in the story? I want my name in.

You just talk about whatever you like, Mrs Wilmot, and of course your name and your husband's name will be in the story.

If you don't mind, I don't want my name in. You can put everything in my wife's name.

Whatever you say, Mr Wilmot.

Father and I have discussed the whole situation and one thing we want you to print is that we didn't work all these years to raise a killer for a son. We never knew he was like this.

Mom! Jesus Christ! Come on, Dad, take her in the kitchen. I don't need this, you don't think I'm under enough strain already? I mean, how can you say that! I didn't do it! Get her out of my sight, Dad.

It's a free country, Chuckie, I'm not leaving.

All right, all right, stay in the room, but please – Mr Molloy has to stay objective, he can't allow emotions—

So you're trying to shut me up.

No. I am *not* trying to shut you up. Ask him anything you want, both of you. Tell him anything. It's just my life, that's all. Nothing to goddamn worry about, nothing but shit – Dad! Where are you going? Come on. You just got here.

You stop that cursing this minute, son, or I'm leaving.

Okay, okay. I'm sorry.

You're getting upset and then you upset me. I can't afford another heart attack, you know that.

I know, right, come on everybody. Let's just relax. I'll make some coffee.

I can't drink coffee.

Well then you don't have to have any, Dad.

As your father I feel I have a right to ask Mr Molloy a question. He sees a lot of these situations. Mr Molloy, have you ever found a pattern among criminal minds? For instance anything that might come from their backgrounds? Because my son had everything a boy could want, so I just can't figure out how he ended up killing someone.

Oh, brother, I might as well just give up right now.

Heavens, don't give up now, Wilmot. Things are just getting interesting.

He is your father, Chuckie. He can ask what he wants. He raised you, he paid the bills.

No, Mom! Just because he's my father doesn't make it right.

Son, just tell us why you did it. Get it off your chest. We won't tell the police.

Dad, please *believe* me: I didn't do it. I need your support, I need you to have faith in me.

But, son, if you didn't do it, who did?

How should *I* know? If I knew, would I be going through all this? Somebody did it, somebody. We all have the same problem: figuring out who. I don't know any more about it than you.

Perhaps you could tell me, Mr and Mrs Wilmot, what makes you think your son killed this young woman?

Molloy, please. I don't know if I can take much more.

I'm not saying you did it, Wilmot. Of course, then again, maybe you did.

Oh, really. What *are* you saying?

I'm interested in why *they* think you did it.

I never understand what the hell you're talking about.

Perhaps what they are thinking about you, we could also think about other people.

Boy. And here I sit, waiting for the axe to come down while you think. Go on. Have a nice little chat the three of you.

Father and I think he killed her because she was going to break up his marriage.

I don't believe this! Do you – I – I – you hear what they're saying? It's not true, I'm telling you! I'm the one who would know. You make me sick, I don't have to put up with any of you.

Why don't you just think about what they're saying?

What's there to think about? That I killed some girl because she was going to break up my marriage? Are you serious? It's so obvious it's dumb. The oldest cliché in the world. Anyway, I've already explained. In my situation it was different. There was a sincere commitment in my situation.

You call that an explanation?

Yes, I do. There was no way I was going to leave M and the kids. No way. That was the deal and that was that.

Something doesn't make sense.

Hey – what do you want from me? I knew what I knew, I knew my own mind and my own thoughts and my own plans.

How can you be so sure of everything, Mr Charles J. Wilmot III?

Because I'm sure! I knew what I was doing. I made the decisions and I stuck to them. That girl didn't mean a hill of beans if you compare her to a lifelong obligation.

Ah, yes. Duty. Obedience. And the girl gets shafted down the Sewanee. But of course you didn't murder her, oh no. You didn't have to. Just little by little reduced her to shit. Good man, Wilmot. Brave fellow. Knight of the golden balls.

Now see here, you just stop making fun of my son, Mr Molloy, and I agree with Mother: both of you are drunk. The language!

We have *not* been drinking, Dad. And why don't you and Mom just shut up so I can finish what I was saying to him, I suppose you're bragging about *your* balls, eh, Molloy? Ha! You know damn well I don't mean 'obligation' like that. It wasn't a burden. It was a *commitment* with Marilyn, a free decision. *That's* the kind of balls *you* don't have. Maybe *you* think sticking to promises is boring and suffocating. I don't. In fact, if you want to know what I think, if you really want to know my philosophy, that's a big part of it, keeping your word. Loyalty. All down the line you stick to what you promise. Isn't that right, Mom? Hey, you're awful quiet over there, come on. I didn't mean to hurt your feelings.

Say something.

Dad, please. I'm still your son. You don't have to look away like that.

Maybe your father—

Hey, would you mind? I'm trying to have a conversation with my parents. You never stop butting in, do you?

I'm still thinking about the other point.

What other point?

That the girl was killed to stop your marriage breaking down. Killed by you, that is. Before she died and again now.

What the hell are you talking about? Mixing up words as usual. Somebody killed her and then she died, that's that. The marriage *wasn't* breaking down and I *didn't* kill her.

Let's say you're telling the truth. Hard to believe, but let's just say you are.

I am.

Okay, but who knew all this besides you, Wilmot? Who else besides you knew what a stupid little hill of beans – pardon me, not *even* a hill of beans – that girl was and what little risk she posed to your marriage?

Umm, well now, let's see, yeah, good point. I would have thought Marilyn would realise. Realise the love between us. And Anna. I didn't really know too many other people, work took up a lot of my time.

But I thought you said Marilyn and Anna didn't know

about the affair before the murder. Get those lies in order, little Chuckie.

They *didn't* know. I meant *afterward*. And your insults won't confuse me. What I meant was, when they *did* find out I would have thought they would know she didn't mean anything. Whereas certainly Marilyn, I wouldn't know about Anna, certainly Marilyn has the reverse idea, that this girl mattered. Now, if you take strangers, yeah, other people wouldn't realise how unimportant she was and might actually have thought I might leave M. for her. But the flaw in that is nobody else knew! That's the thing, that's what I keep saying and that's what I can't figure out, why the police suspect Anna and Marilyn. As if they knew anything about it. It would have to be someone who knew—

And cared.

Well, yeah, I suppose. Or maybe just a random thing. Just a coincidence. It does happen. A thing can be a coincidence.

Oh, come on. You really still believe you kept this relationship a secret from Anna and Marilyn? The two people who knew you best, knew your schedule, everything? The two people with the most to lose?

Yes, I do, and I'll never change my mind.

You are a stupid man.

And you're a piece of shit.

All right, Chuckie. Now you've done it. We're leaving. Come on, Father.

My own son is a disgrace.

Dad, I'm sorry. Please. It's just that I'm under too much stress. I'm not myself. Mom. Don't go.

The two of you did not need to say 'bastard' and 'shit'.

Okay, okay, I agree.

Have you told him about your affair with Anna? That dead girl wasn't the first, Mr Molloy.

Oh, Chuckie, Chuckie, bad boy.

Stop it right now, Mom. There is no need to bring that up. My so-called 'affair' with Anna. Ignore her, Molloy.

Oh, no! Ignore her? Why, what your mother just said is very interesting. And doesn't it just go to show what a fascinating hill of fucking beans life can be. So maybe that *is* why you killed the girl, to help everybody hold on to what they had. Only now the three of you have lost it all anyway. So sad.

You don't need much to get going, do you, Molloy? I *never* had an affair with Anna, let's get the record straight. My mother brings this up every chance she gets no matter what I say. And by the way, why *do* you, Mom? I've never understood that and I think I have a right to know. I think it's about time we cleared the air.

To learn from our mistakes. You didn't learn from Anna, you went and did it again. So I have to make you go back over it.

What is this? Kindergarten?

You were in love with Anna and you had an affair with her, Chuckie. And then you got rid of her.

Don't be absurd! It's all in your mind! Come on, Molloy, you tell them it's not true – did Anna tell you we had an affair?

Not yet.

You know something? You're an irritating son of a bitch.

And I can't imagine what that girl saw in you, Charles J. Wilmot III. Every time you open your mouth you spit on her.

I was good to her! You've got some nerve, as if I treat people like dirt.

You do. That girl cared for you – and probably Anna, too – and now you have no problem throwing them in the garbage.

My chest – my heart—

Sit down, Dad. It's all right. Come on, Molloy, it upsets them how we're talking.

How do they feel about murder? Like that any better?

I said that's enough!

I'm sorry, Dad. Don't cry. I'll do anything to make it up to you. We'll figure it out, it'll blow over.

Mr Molloy is asleep again, Chuckie, and I really have to get Father home. You're making him very ill. Do you have any laundry?

Leave it, it's okay, you're tired.

Are you going to be all right?

I'll be fine, I'm fine.

I didn't mean anything, son. I love you.

I know, Dad. Just look after yourself. Molloy! For Christ sake you could at least say goodbye to them.

Goodbye? Oh, yes. That's all that's left now, goodbye goodbye, charming to meet two more just like him.

Well, thank you very much, Mr Molloy. We don't get many compliments lately. The neighbours won't talk to us.

I wouldn't thank him for that, Dad.

We'll see you soon, Chuckie. The children are fine.

Okay. Bye. You'll come tomorrow?

Tomorrow.

Right. Bye.

Yeah, and as for you, get the hell out of my house.

You're not *in* your house, pal. You lost it. Remember?

Jesus Christ! The minute you leave, which is right now, I'm phoning your paper to make a complaint. Reporter my ass. This whole thing is outrageous. I don't know what your angle is, but you've got some kind of mental imbalance and I don't want to see you around here again.

Don't worry. Give you another chance to defecate? Never.

Get out, you bastard.

31

Molloy. You hear me? Hey, all of you, get lost, this is not a peep show. Molloy. That's it, let me lift you. Can you stand up? Okay, we sit. What I say, you scum? Leave! How *you* feel, somebody stare at you? Huh? Good riddance. See how *you* like it, end up in the gutter one of these days, no more high and mighty!

Miguelito?

I here, Molloy.

Where?

Third Avenue. You said Third Avenue, and boy, I tell you, Third Avenue is one long place.

I said?

Yeah, to me, you better believe it.

I – I'm not well.

Who you telling, Molloy? You look like a strung-out addict. I told you not to leave, you not well and your arms didn't heal over, and I been up and down this Third Avenue, up and down, you could have been dead by now. I'm disgusted with you.

Help me.

Yeah, but I not finished with you. The fright of my life, Molloy, you know what could happen, lying in a drain on Third Avenue? Do you? Or you not living in this world? Wake up! I talking to you!

Why am I here?

That's what I want to know. Front of Tower Records, you into records or something?

Records?

Yeah, 63rd and Third, Molloy. Every street on Third Avenue, you name it, I been there. So why this one?

63rd.

Molloy. You not listening to me. I am pissed at you. Hear that? You care? You putting danger in you self, man, and you got me running up and down this fucking place because I got a bad feeling about death coming after you and I'm trying to get to you first.

I'm sick.

Hey. Don't tell me this again. You already fainted, you shouldn't have ever got up from the table. And now look.

If I just eat something.

You gonna eat all right, I make sure about that, and we got to look at those cuts and get you a bath, you smell like a piece of garbage. Where you live, Molloy?

Live?

Jesus Christ, Molloy. I trying to help you get home. You want to sleep in this sewer?

You're not going to my apartment, Miguelito, if that's what you're thinking.

Oh, now that wakes you up. And you bet I am thinking that, because I am going to feed you a decent meal and put you to bed.

Bed? What time is it? What's the time? Anyone! Tell me the time! I've got to know the time!

It's four o'clock, Molloy, come on, we—

Only eight hours, Miguelito! Eight hours! The day is over in eight hours, gone again, I can't go to sleep, there's no time, got to figure it out, figure it out, get there, stop it—

Hold on, Molloy! Hold on! Don't run! I'll help you, I've got you – Tomas! Hold the door. Tell him your address,

Molloy. Go on, before you faint, oh Tomas, I think he's going to faint. Molloy! Open your eyes! This is my friend's taxi, he been driving me around after you. Say you address to him, Molloy. Come on!

48th and Ninth. Hurry.

Okay, Tomas. Go.

Time, Miguelito. Time.

Lean back, Molloy. You cannot keep you head up. Against my arm. I'm sorry I yell at you, I'm sorry. That's it, close your eyes. I can't take this, Tomas.

He gonna be sick, Miguelito.

Just get him home.

The traffic. Every fucking street.

You drive safe, Tomas. Molloy got too much danger already. You waking up again, Molloy? That's it. You can cry now. Let it come out of you.

By tomorrow too late. Always too late.

You right, Jackie Molloy, you got to do it today. For you it's today or else. Oh, I feel it, I feel it too much, up and down Third Avenue. These is not just tears for this day, these is tears for the end of this day.

32

The rain begins slowly and then pours from the dark sky as the taxi approaches Jackie's building.

Jackie's tears have come like these torrents. The moments of consciousness on Third Avenue, heaped upon hours battling the voracious Amazon, have nearly broken him. Miguelito and Tomas help Jackie out of the cab and shelter him against the onslaught.

Nearing the entrance to the building, Jackie suddenly claws at his arms. Dereliction, dereliction, bleed bleed you failure, you scum, you maggot, omission, commission, too little too late, hours are all you have left, rats in the alley count for more than you. Miguelito and Tomas pin Jackie's arms behind and rush him indoors. Jackie has forgotten he will not allow Miguelito upstairs. He cannot manage alone.

Miguelito and Tomas support him up the four flights. Jackie points to his door and Tomas leaves to buy food.

Nothing Miguelito has seen or known of Jackie Molloy before this day prepares him for the squalor.

Remains of 1959, papers, bags, and boxes heaped and scattered, disgorged from bloated cupboards. Mouldy food, plates, pans, days upon days attacked and infested by flies and roaches. An encrusted hotplate, frayed cord, bare bulb.

Light from the one window is snuffed out beneath a layer of black grime.

Miguelito begins to weep. He guides his broken friend to the mattress sinking into its springs, and helps him stretch out. He stands alone in the middle of the dank and dark, covers his face not to retch.

Jackie cannot lift his head, but turns and looks at Miguelito.

I told you not to come.

This what you think of yourself, Molloy? Filth?

Jackie turns away.

Get out, Miguelito. Nobody asked you.

You know something, Molloy? I got no time to stand around waiting for people to ask.

Oh, don't you now?

And you want to know why?

I don't want to know any fucking thing from you, Miguelito. I told you to leave.

Oh, thanking you, master, I never thought you'd ask. Well, I got HIV, Molloy. You understand? I got death creeping up on me every day, the big fucking sneak. So everything I got to say, I say it now, man, and I don't give a shit if you don't like it, because you got a type of HIV, too, you got a nice and sneaky little worm like a piece of HIV swimmin' around in you all slow and quiet and then – bam! Got you! So I can ask whatever I want, Molloy, and I am asking you: is this room what you think you made of you life? Huh? You think you made turds and that's it?

Jackie hauls himself up on his elbows, shaking.

That's right, you fucking fairy. And you think I give a shit about any of it? Come down from the clouds with your fancy HIV, take a good look. This is how it is. This is how it was. It's called the real world. Now get out. I've got things to do.

Jackie falls back on the bed.

What things, Molloy? Who you kidding? What more can you do? You body is collapsed on you, man, it won't go. Oh, sure, you make fun where I stick my cock. But what happened to yours, my Molloy? Huh? You could be such a beautiful man. But you got to forgive youself.

Jackie covers his face. Wretchedness in a pair of puny hands that never held the real thing. Fingers good only for letting it slip through.

Miguelito has tissues in his pocket. He wipes a pan, boils water in it. Wipes again, boils again. He discovers the tea towel he washed for Jackie late last night, early this morning. He sits beside Jackie who refuses to show himself and rolls up the sleeves of his putrid shirt. He carefully dabs the wounds, opened again on the way into the building and now weeping softly. He immerses the towel in the scalding water and pulls it out with a fork to let it air. Then wraps it around Jackie's right arm. In a few moments he repeats the procedure and wraps the left.

A knock on the door: Tomas. Miguelito admits him. He is carrying two brown-paper bags.

There is no table, one chair. Tomas clears a space on the floor and rests himself against the wall.

Miguelito sits in the chair beside Jackie with a cardboard container.

Jackie, bring you arms down. You got to eat this. Bit at a time. Small.

Light broth with delicate slivers of chicken.

Jackie sits up and eats all of this, one spoonful after another, very slowly.

Miguelito looks at Tomas, Tomas nods.

Jackie, says Miguelito, listen to me: I got a doctor's appointment. Tomas will stay with you. I told him you not to leave this house, and he's like me, he means business. We got more food here and Tomas he will give you some and you got to eat it. I be back two hours, three hours.

Hand me those papers over there.
These?
Yes. When you come back I want you to read them to me.
Okay.
Miguelito.
What?
Are you sick?
No, Molloy. Not yet.

33

The food has helped. Jackie lies back and stares at the ceiling. Tomas, resting against the wall, is a still and gentle presence. Miguelito, too, even in departure, continues to hover over and contain the terrors in Jackie's dungeon.

And so he is able, on tiptoes, for he can hardly take more effort, to approach. The first time in thirty-five years to come close to his blindness. To re-enter lost opportunity, the darkest endless hole. Wherein arrogance suffocates light and knowledge.

Now, 1994, the swagger on its knees, Jackie is drawn up and on to the flaked discoloured ceiling and enters a photograph. A scene fixed at a crossroads. Before a wrong choice. He is wide-eyed on his back on his bed, he is in the picture again. At last, not too late after all, not disappeared, there he is at the centre. He has emerged from the shadows, courage to see and be seen, he is no longer the blurred background floating in distances while others take shape.

He is waiting outside the No Name. Waiting for Chuck and the girl. No pressure, no urgency. The usual time, the usual situation. Casual. Jackie Molloy in command.

He remembers waiting like this for Sarah and David Mulligan. The experience with them should have tipped him off, too, for now something in the memory resonates. He knew them so well and felt so comfortable with them that he no longer hid, no longer feared losing track of them or being noticed. Their routine was clear and consistent. Jackie blended in seamlessly. Confident of every angle, every possibility, every outcome.

Perhaps he recalls them now because the time waiting at the No Name yielded an unexpected, unprepared-for turn in the road. Just as one occasion waiting for the Mulligans outside their favourite restaurant. A turn passed by. Where did that come from, not in the plan, drive on.

The usual pattern: David arrived first. He became impatient. Sarah was late. Jackie didn't mind at all. He liked to see David frustrated.

Finally she raced up to him, out of breath and full of false apologies. She had met friends at an opening at a gallery, they stayed on, didn't notice the time, and so on. David jabbed his watch, threw his hands in the air, accused, berated. Sarah stared impassively. Finally she said, Are you finished? Because I think I am. David's jaw was set. Jackie thought: you better pay attention, you stupid bastard, or you'll lose her. Sarah then said, simply: This is the last time you will ever speak to me that way. David retorted: And the last time you will choose your friends over me. They eyed each other like chess players. Entered the restaurant in silence.

Jackie waited. Oh, David, he thought, you have made a big mistake. I have overheard all the talk about *your* future, *your* plans, *your* dreams, and Sarah has never faltered in her loyalty. No questions, no jealousy, no interference. Only support. And now when she wants the same? A big mistake, David. *I* wouldn't have made that mistake.

After almost twenty minutes, Jackie went into the restaurant. He leaned against the doorway and perused the tables, pretending to search for someone. Gloating over David's failure to satisfy Sarah.

Then – so many times for Jackie the problem is *then* – Sarah looked at him. She left David sitting at their table and approached. Jackie saw her nearing as one might see a mirage wobbling on the surface of a desert, like that unexpected turn in the road, this is not real, there is no one there, no one coming toward me.

But suddenly the illusion became Sarah Mulligan and she said, I am the woman who phoned for the taxi, I'll just get my coat.

And by the time she returned to go off with Jackie Molloy, Jackie Molloy had become the apparition. A swirling quaking non-existence blowing down the street to the concrete ballast of the *Mirror* building.

The evening outside the No Name Jackie felt the same understanding of air.

As he saw rising towards him from out of the footpath the unmistakable figure of Anna Laskowski.

She passed within inches, imparting a distinctive aroma that lingered as she looked for a place to lie in wait. And carrying a familiar tightness around the eyes and mouth, sending a shudder through Jackie Molloy.

Now the crossroads loom: the fork where absence and presence diverge.

And in the first step towards the fateful choice, Jackie felt himself disappear. Disbelief reduced him to vapour like a magic wand, poof, do not see, won't believe, I'll go away.

Eventually Chuck and the girl arrived, as they were bound to do, no way around the story now. Anna tucked herself in at the side of a news-stand, and with steel ball-bearing eyes, followed them down the stairs into the bar.

Here was another moment. Another chance. For taking back the first step, I didn't mean to go that way, now I see where I must diverge, clear the way, let me through, I see I see, I am here.

At this Godforsaken crossroads, alone in the wilderness of

remain or flee, cringing while cougars approach the feast, no help, no hope, what else but the same story over and over unto black infinity, Jackie Molloy did not step into light but floated further into his first commitment, to be away and gone in darkness.

1994: Retract, retract, didn't mean, didn't want.

And Jackie on his ceiling walks past the unsuspecting Anna, into the No Name and over to Chuck and the girl who are seated at their usual table. He is calm, he speaks with authority.

You don't know me, but I know you – I'll explain later, I am not ashamed – and I have to tell you, I have to warn you, Anna Laskowski is waiting outside, she has observed you together. I am afraid for your lives, yes, I mean it, please believe me, nothing less than that, presence versus absence, that is why I am here, presence is at risk, I see things, you will not be allowed to remain, and yes, I finally admit to seeing things about you, too, oh, please, do I have to say it, the love I see, there, now it's out, it's named for all time, your love your love, I know I know, I have faced it. You must go. Without doubt, hesitation, go quickly. She is waiting. When, where, how it will happen, I can only dread. But we can stop her if you leave and run away. Listen carefully: I will step back outside. I will divert her. Somehow. And you, both of you, take these tickets, please, take them, a flight on Pan Am leaving Idlewild tonight, any flight, take off. I will handle the rest, Anna, Marilyn, don't worry, oh, you do not want absence, no, let me tell you about absence, the state of walking talking death, you do not want, you do not – So you'll take the tickets? Thank God! Give me half an hour, then – Go! Go! You'll see the fork in the road, airplanes, jasmine, magic carpets line the way, you'll make no mistake, Go! No, don't thank me, I am on my knees thanking *you*! You have saved my life, yes, it is true, for I saw, I knew, and you let me carry out in time.

In the midst of the garbage of aftermath, 1994, Tomas rocks Jackie and the sobs pass over him and out like tides.

34

Miguelito returns, six thirty p.m. Five and a half hours left.

Tomas rises from Jackie's bedside.

You okay?

Miguelito shrugs, says nothing.

Tell me, Miguelito.

But the young man puts a finger to his lips and closes his eyes.

Seal the naming of horrors until the final note has played, until the music stops and the scramble for the last chair leaves you standing. Only then unleash the words that make it so, your place is gone, the time of you is up, put off put off until the very last nightingale.

Tomas begins to cry. Miguelito shakes his head, no, no, not yet, Tomas, let in too soon you won't survive.

Jackie has been watching and listening. He says nothing as Miguelito sits beside him and takes up the stack of papers. Tomas returns cross-legged to the floor, his head bowed.

The vigil begins.

Hey, I thought you weren't coming back.

Why wouldn't I?

Be honest, I mean, isn't the subject supposed to just

answer the goddamn questions, you know, get things moving along, bam-bam-bam, A to B to C – Wow! – There's my old friend ABC Freight again, the most IMPORTANT company in the world. See? Like right there I went off the subject.

Oh, I don't think so, Mrs Wilmot.

I did! That's my whole problem, I don't stick to the point. But I'm trying, I really am. When I wake up in the mornings, well, you know, twelve or whatever, I do twenty sit-ups – seriously, I'm getting a pot-belly, don't say you haven't noticed, so I'm on a diet, too – so I do twenty sit-ups and I have a certain thing I say over and over: Focus yourself, Marilyn, stick to your goal.

Goal?

Yeah. Purpose.

And what would that be?

I'll tell you. And then you'll be the only person besides me who knows because everybody would laugh at me, I mean it, they would. They think I've lost everything. Fine. But I haven't. Okay: the purpose of all this, the sit-ups, the diet, the concentration, is to get those kids of mine back. Right here, back with me, where they belong. You understand?

Yes. I do.

If people think I'm going to crack, they're wrong. I've never cracked before and every day of my life with C. Wilmot, boy, let me tell you, if I didn't crack then I won't crack now. And then after the kids are home I'm going to sue the one and only Mr C. Wilmot Bastard, his goddamn MOTHER, AND every social worker in New York State for breach or whatever without even giving me a trial. I want those kids' college fees, money for clothes, food, you name it. A new car, bikes for all of them.

I wish you a lot of luck.

You want to know something? I knew you would. Don't

ask me why, I just had this feeling you wouldn't laugh at me.

It's not funny.

Hey – you mind if I ask you something?

No.

You're not a very happy guy, are you?

That's one way to put it.

That's exactly how I'd put it and I was just thinking you look sick, too. Lost a lot of weight since the last time.

I, no, I guess I haven't been feeling well. A cold – I've had a cold. Can't seem to shake it.

A cold? Come on. A cold doesn't make you look like that. Your face reminds me of – like in the old novels, those creepy ones, 'the hollow cheeks, the sunken red-rimmed eyes' – CONSUMPTION! That's it. That's the word I was looking for, like what they always got in Dickens, where you waste away. Do you have a fever?

I don't think so.

Maybe a chill. Well, you better watch it. A person can get down to skin and bones in no time. Hey, you know what I think, I think we need a little something to warm us up. What do you say?

Jesus, you look terrible. *I'll* decide. Let me see now. YES. We *do* need a little something. Scotch? Gin?

Scotch.

Now you're talking! Boy, we're living in a time of complete social upheaval, aren't we? You hardly know what to believe any more.

That was quick. Refill?

There. I like a person who knows what's what. My other goal for when the kids are back is to figure out my beliefs and pass them on to the next generation. So they have something to hold on to. This back and forth, up and down, not knowing one day to the next what's going on, it's for the birds. Hey, by the way – does this have anything to do with the story? The murder?

This what?

This right here. You and me. Drinking and talking. It feels great, but I really meant it when I said I'm trying to concentrate, so I just need to know: are we on track?

She's dead. The pressure on her neck sent blood out of her eyes.

Yeah! Whoopee, how about that!

Indeed. And there is the answer to your question. Everything seems to be going along just fine, all according to plan.

What are you getting at, wiseguy?

She's dead, Mrs Wilmot, and as far as I can tell, that fact doesn't upset you very much.

Now wait a minute, that doesn't mean I WANTED that bitch to get killed. Or that I DID it.

But you let it happen. At the very least. Even though you knew her.

I did not know her! What the hell are you up to?

Just checking. Somehow I had this ridiculous notion that you arranged to meet her once in a coffee shop. With Anna Laskowski.

Oh, brother. Wow. Now I get it. I mean, you – this is really—

But obviously I'm wrong.

Wrong doesn't even come close, buddy-boy. Jesus Christ! What kind of a person do you think I am, you think I could sit here like this if I *knew* her? Even if I detested her! Loathed her! Which I did! Just sit here la-dee-da, not a care in the old world?

Oh, yes. You could and you are. So am I. The difference is you're *glad* she got killed.

So I'm supposed to take that to mean you knew her, too? I don't believe this – here, give me your glass, I'll top it up. And how about you, Marilyn? Why, I don't mind if I do.

I knew her 'too'?

Don't try to trick me! You know what I mean.

Oh, yes, I certainly do.

Whose side are you on anyway? That bitch ruined my life! She took my family! What's supposed to happen to ME now? Let's hear the answer to that one if you're so smart.

You *gave* your family away. You're a whiner. A lazy complainer. She won and you couldn't stand it. You didn't even *like* Mr C. Wilmot Bastard.

So what! He was *mine*. That bitch took something that belonged to me, and lazy my ass, I bet she didn't do twenty sit-ups her whole life, the only thing she ever did was rob something that wasn't hers.

And the hell with the fact that what she took was of no use to you anyway, no value.

Exactly. The point is *stealing. Taking.*

But now the children are gone. You expected to destroy that girl's life without having to pay, didn't you? The same charge you level against her. Oh, sweet Jesus, isn't logic a marvellous toy.

It's *not* the same thing! You're playing games again. You're trying to make me admit I killed her when I didn't.

Oh, heavens, no! Of course you didn't. How could I say such a thing. We were all just standing around minding our own business when all of a sudden a young girl none of us knew or cared about got her throat caught in a belt.

Jesus Christ. You want some advice? Maybe you ought to forget your goddamn story and just check into the looney bin. I'm beginning to think there's something weird going on here – oh, shit, who the hell could that be? – You know the last time somebody banged on my door like that? Besides you, I mean. The last time was the MOTHER.

The SOCIAL WORKER. But it can't be them, there's nothing left to take. Coming! Coming! Hold your fucking horses! Pour us another one there, Mr Reporter, and when I get back I'll help you do what you're *supposed* to be doing: REPORT. About time, don't you think? Ouch! I'm always stubbing my toe on that goddamn table—

If only there were such a thing as obliteration. Not just imposters like forgetting. Then in Jackie's bones there would be no creaks of recall. Of who appeared at Marilyn Wilmot's door as he was pouring himself another drink and congratulating the ace reporter from the *Mirror* for pulling the cotton wool over—

Oh sweet Jesus, look who's HERE, he's HERE, my BABY, you came back to me, hold me, oh my big BOY, are you all right—

And the big boy Bobby Wilmot nearly falls into the house, he has been running, he has run away from his grandparents' in his suit and tie and leather shoes and he can hardly stand, he is reeling under the strain of shirt and collar. Miguelito continues to read, but Jackie is now beyond words, in the realm of what signifies. For the bottle of Scotch is nearly empty, glasses strew the table, shoes and socks underneath, and the tape recorder whirs in eavesdrop.

Bobby gapes. From the table to the man to the mother.

It's okay, baby, he's a REPORTER, he's going to help us all get back together again, he knows I didn't do it, and then we'll be fine, oh sweetie I've missed you so much.

But the boy Bobby is staring at the man Jackie. Jackie is looking, too. He shouldn't, for eyes are the unforgettable, especially Bobby's astigmatism, yet the alcohol limbers the nerve to stare for it also carries Jackie away. Here and gone, all in one, blessed absence to accompany presence, an escort for Jackie when he must appear.

Anyhow, look all you want, this child is surely too young, too new, to apprehend disgrace. Surely his mind has by now disinfected itself of the base, craven louse found in the bushes, and would pick it off again without a moment's recognition.

But, no. Bobby does not flinch. He studies the shame arising from the man from the bushes who is now in his mother's house. And holds him with a gaze of the deepest sorrow and compassion. As a much older person of great assuredness. As if what he sees can be accepted. Forgiven.

Jackie twists in his chair, this lack of judgement a bizarre sentence that rips open his grief. Tears, tears, there will be no end, you do not know what I have done, you do not know what I have seen.

Marilyn rocks on the floor and pines for her son. He turns from Jackie. Enfolds her in his arms, kisses her lips and her hair.

Jackie runs from this house, certain – no, far more than certain, he is riveted to the conviction, brought about by the power of legs in flight – that he can elude the place. Oh poor poor, can't you hear, fate is laughing, there *is* nowhere to go but the place of in and down.

All choice over, he collides with the very stream he had determined would not thaw and carry him to meet another.

Past swirls like fingerpaint into present. Correspondences of times arriving and gone by.

35

Oh Jackie that's so good for your Georgie don't stop don't stop.

And Jackie Molloy aged thirteen is about to ejaculate, twitching, trembling, beguiled by his own hardness, his throbbing tumid wilfulness. The build-up, the heightening to unheard-of pleasure and release.

He cannot imagine what happens to Georgie. But each time he arches his back she rides hard against his buttocks and moans or cries out, and when she suddenly begins to run her fingers through his hair in a frenzy, he knows that she too is about to let loose something like his ejaculation, so he rides himself in time with her, Now Jackie now, do it to Georgie

But in the way of almost almost and nearly there, now was not to be and never. The only remnant a fleeting glimpse, surrounded in darkness, of ecstasies slipping from the pinnacle.

And the sound – how can this be described, such a delicate meeting and parting of steel components – a turning doorknob. If only a lock or a latch, oh what mortals wouldn't sacrifice for golden ramparts, bulwarks, turrets and moats. But castles are dreams, Jackie Molloy, the joke is on you, those princesses, knights, and trysts.

For Mick Molloy is coming through the door, a simple twist of hardware and he is in.

And sees the ransacked chamber, Georgie gasping, scrambling off the back of his son, struggling to cover her betrayal with a flimsy cloth. Too late.

The first blow slams her to the floor, the second her skull against the sink. And then the snapping of arms and Jackie lies stark. His nakedness rigid like a cadaver, oh please die, be dead be dead to Georgie, these are no longer the cries of a Georgie but howls rung from the throes of extinction as she is hoisted. And dashed into graffiti against the wall, with the father wheezing and gagging as if he were loading crates on the dock.

Suddenly, how can impetus be explained, there is no way Jackie Molloy can refuse admission to Georgie's supplications, desperate desperate pounding on every door. He is about to vomit, his muscles are in seizure and the laments rend him.

He explodes from the bed, as Georgie, face down in red streaks, tries to scrape her way towards the door. Until the punch of a large foot lifts and drops her like a sack and her chest rattles and drains from her mouth. And then the boy is all over the man, kicking, biting, clawing, hitting. Rage rumbles from Jackie Molloy like a locomotive, gathering gaining speed and force, and his father tumbles backwards, shock freezing his face, as Jackie falls on Georgie, hugs the pieces, drags, shouts, Run! Run!

And does not see his father rise and come to him from behind.

Slam him, bend him, pin him at the edge of the table, you want to know how, this is how, and shove into him, too big for you, isn't it, can't take it, stretch stretch, rip the tissue, rupture vessels, make Jackie, make him take in, and sensation goes cold, apertures harden, as the father rams and rams and finally pours himself at will into inside Jackie Molloy.

Oh Georgie Georgie who was once a person not a thing

like you, she is tucked away and safe in nothingness, yours is the torture now, Georgie Georgie from the embers of mementoes in the time and place of re-enactment.

36 ʃ

Futilities: concealed to the last. The cruelty of choice, the using up of chances.

13 March 1959, no reason to hear the clock ticking, Jackie follows Chuck and the girl to Penn Station. Four p.m. She has never accompanied him there. But this is Sunday, the usual commuters are absent. The couple have taken the chance that no one they know from work will pass through. They have spent the day in the girl's apartment. Chuck told Marilyn he had to work, and now he is returning to Farmyard Lane.

Long Island Railroad, Platform 32. There is only one question in Jackie's mind since the note outside the apartment building: 'Please' what? He is wracked from hurling himself through the maze of this story trying to find the answer. He has decided that if the girl could say more, she would. Therefore it serves no purpose, and perhaps even frightens and upsets her, for Jackie to be visible. It is up to him to work out what she wants. His fault, after all, that the Valentine was lost.

So today he is a businessman wearing a suit, propping a newspaper under his arm, and carrying a briefcase. On his head a hat like Harry Truman's. He has told Marty he needs several weeks off to tend a dying relation, and Marty is elated.

Jackie must watch very carefully for clues. There is no more chance at words, he is sure the notes are over. All that remains is the decision to act.

Out of his turmoil in the maze, Jackie has come to believe that the girl is trying to communicate one of two things: either she wants help for herself, or she wants help for Chuck. He cannot imagine another possibility. Chuck doesn't know about Jackie, so she can't be asking him to help them both, together.

Today he is alert for any indication that might point him in the right direction. He hopes the girl will not ask him to protect Chuck. He will if he must. He cannot deny her wishes. But Jackie Molloy dearly and truly longs only to save and possess *her* and leave Chuck to his fate. For he has also come to believe that the girl will not, cannot, kill her lover. And so the deed falls to Anna and Marilyn, once they realise the girl has betrayed them.

Before they make this discovery, Jackie must rescue the girl and take her away. He hopes – he believes – that this is the response the girl wants of him.

The train for Hempstead leaves at four forty. Chuck and the girl sit at a counter and drink coffee. There is no pleasure in their outing, no hope contained in the imminent parting.

But to Jackie's surprise, Chuck is by far the more anxious of the two. The girl puts a hand on his shoulder, whispers, adds sugar to his coffee and stirs it for him. He is wringing his hands, holding his head, nearly distraught.

In contrast, the girl appears strong and calm. She is reassuring Chuck. She makes several important points gesturing with her hands, as if she is putting a third party on notice. Her loyalty to Chuck is obvious.

Jackie feels nauseous with envy and steadies himself by leaning against a kiosk. I must do what she asks, I must do what she asks, and he realises, seeing Chuck's despondency, that the required course of action is becoming clearer and is almost upon him, the dreaded option is the one she is requesting. Of course: the girl has been pleading for Chuck, not for herself. She is free. But Chuck is owned by Marilyn, the children, Farmyard Lane and ABC Freight – Anna Laskowski? Chuck is the one at risk. The enormity of that risk has entered the girl and she is passing the responsibility to me because she cannot follow him to Levittown herself.

Oh, dear God, am I to accompany him and save him? Stop the murder? I don't want to! But will she ever forgive me if I fail? If she discovers that I too want him dead? Dead is too strong, I only want him out of the way. And if that is not to be, if she sees me only as a friend, a protector of Chuck, an ally in her deception – how will the pain be borne?

Four thirty. They rise from their stools. Chuck puts some coins on the counter. Suddenly Jackie feels he must let the girl know he is near and will accompany Chuck. What use the whole exercise if she is unaware of his presence? He removes his hat and stands in full view as she and her lover walk away from the snack bar. Surely she will see him now.

The concern is unnecessary. As the girl passes, a piece of paper flutters to the floor at Jackie's feet.

She and Chuck kiss at the entrance to Track 32 without another word. She retreats from the crowd. A look of fear, fear she hid from Chuck. Eyes darting around the station, she quickly disappears into the Ladies Room.

Jackie is dizzy with euphoria, she sees me, she sees me. He reaches down and picks up the note.

How will I ever thank you, please stay near.

The crossroads is reached, signs interpreted, a path chosen.

Jackie boards the four forty to Hempstead.

And thus it is and forever will be.

That he does not observe the girl emerge from the Ladies Room and search in vain for the missing Jackie Molloy.

37

From a grimy window Chuck stares at the blackness beneath Penn Station. The train jerks and screeches out of the tunnel and finally emerges into a pale smog blanketing factories and tenements near the railyards. And casting an eerie light across the 4.40.

Jackie sits in an aisle seat several rows behind Chuck. Near a door so he can exit first. He re-reads the girl's note and feels a soft calm spread over him like bathwater. His disdain for Chuck recedes as he nestles in the girl's warmth and appreciation. He will do whatever is necessary to save her lover, anything to sustain this tranquility, this lake of peace and well-being. The sensation that he is actually being held. Chuck is no longer a threat, no longer an object of envy, for he will never be able to take away what Jackie and the girl have shared.

The possibility that he might fail this girl is suddenly a nightmare of another era. At this moment Jackie would have to strain his memory to recollect the dread that has pursued him for many weeks. In the flash of a small bit of white paper the panic is gone. Transformation of reality is total, confidence complete. He has managed after all to retrieve the message from the lost Valentine. He has come to the girl in the way and at the time she needed.

The train pulls into Hempstead Station. Jackie disembarks

ahead of Chuck and quickly takes the first taxi. He watches Chuck enter a queue as the few remaining cabs pick up passengers and drive off.

Dropped at Farmyard Lane, the businessman's hat back on his head, Jackie strolls along the street as if it were the Champs-Elysées. He nods and smiles to curious passers-by who cannot place the stranger who acts as if he is on his way home. Indeed, Jackie Molloy has never before now known the power of ownership. The authority of belonging.

Several small children and their mothers occupy the playground. It is nearing time to go in and make supper, so Jackie won't have long to wait. He sits on a bench with his newspaper. Gradually the young families disperse, leaving him on his own, 143 in perfect view. No sign that anyone is there. Jackie will await Chuck's arrival from the bench. For he no longer has any intention of hiding. He is legitimate. His presence has been requested.

Here comes Chuck now. Yes. He has shared a taxi with three other men. The driver drops them several houses down from 143. Chuck is limp, as if he has been across a desert. One of his companions takes his arm and says something, but Chuck shakes his head, no, and walks on alone.

Jackie feels nothing for this man. Chuck's suffering leaves him cold, he is only here to do a job. For her, not for him. All intensity and purpose now flow into the one significance: the agreement with the girl. Understanding that has unleashed in Jackie Molloy a staggering rush of potency.

He observes Chuck Wilmot at the door of his house. Locked. Marilyn and the children have probably gone shopping. Chuck searches his pockets for the key, didn't expect to need it. Finds it, lets himself in.

All quiet for the moment. The girl seems to have suspected, or at least worried, that Chuck might be killed tonight. The Valentine probably even mentioned the 13th and that is why the note today thanked Jackie.

But Jackie Molloy is thinking carefully and does not agree that this is the day. Or the place. Neither seems quite right. However, what he thinks is not the point. The girl has asked for Chuck to be guarded. Asked Jackie to shield him against danger. It could be days before the actual attempt on his life is made. In the meantime, it is Jackie's task to remain alert and vigilant at every moment.

Thus he becomes aware of a group of children staring at him. The children whisper. Cling to each other. Point. But do not giggle.

Jackie searches the playground. What are they looking at?

In the midst of fantasy Jackie Molloy has forgotten about reality. Has not been able to see that they do not match. The suit that is too small, the tight hat stuck on the top of his head like a strange plant. The frayed shirt and stained tie. The briefcase that was once a schoolbag.

He stands up stiffly. At attention.

May I help you?

The children scatter.

Jackie is panic-stricken: they will tell their parents.

But this is no time to run. He cannot. And by God, he *will* not. He is committed. He will simply stroll some more, and if anyone raises questions, he will say he has an appointment with Mr and Mrs Wilmot – an insurance salesman, that's it. Here to sell insurance to the Wilmots.

On second thought, too many neighbours are out on the street. I'll stay here. If something suspicious takes place, I can reach the house quickly enough.

Jackie repositions himself on the bench, breathes deeply, and returns without difficulty to his state of contentment.

Dusk. 13 March 1959. A pleasant evening boding well for swings, sandbox. Gentle hues brushing the rows and rows. This is not the dangerous evening the girl imagined.

When suddenly two figures, not previously on the footpath, appear at the far end of Farmyard Lane. Walking toward 143. Jackie's attention is riveted to this pair, something is not right, every muscle is taut. An involuntary alarm has sounded and his body is on call, emergency emergency.

The two are approaching 143.

What am I seeing? How can this be?

They are making their way up the path to the door. With stealth.

Stealth because glancing, turning, watching. Not in the way of calm light crossing softly into darkness. Jackie is rigid. Shocked.

This is not happening.

I will not allow this to happen!

Anna and Marilyn. Anna and Marilyn.

Jackie bolts from the park with his precious schoolbag just as the two women open the door to 143. Before they go inside they check the neighbourhood again, heads darting like birds. Houses, lawns, and paths are basked in shades of approaching night that cast nuances over Farmyard Lane, and now these two. In their ominous black encapsulated silence they move through the dream like a torpedo.

They have gone into the house.

Jackie moves quickly and finds a place to crouch under the front window. He does not even consider whether he has been seen. His mouth is parched, he can hardly swallow. His lips stick together, sweat bursts from his forehead, his teeth begin to chatter. The girl was right: Anna and Marilyn are going to kill Chuck tonight. Where is confidence at the moment of death? I must stop them.

No sound. They must have gone into the kitchen.

It is nearly dark. Soon Jackie will have the cover of night and can move safely around to the back door. Almost no space separates the neighbour's house, but Jackie cannot think about other eyes looking out of other windows.

Eternity of waiting and damnation, never again let me be so sure of anything.

Jackie waits two more minutes, can bear no more, and crawls around the side of the house, hardly able to contain the din in his chest.

Still no sound. Where the hell *are* they?

Jackie now realises that he may have to enter the house by the front door.

But then he hears it open and bang.

He races on hands and knees back toward where he came from, convinced he has failed. Expecting to see Anna and Marilyn running from the scene, too late too late and now dear God in Heaven what will I tell the girl?

But no! Look! Oh mercy mercy all is not lost! It's *Chuck*!

He has banged the door once and now jerks it open and bangs it again, sound of firecrackers, and then stomps down the path, down Farmyard Lane, around the bend, and out of Island Trees.

Jackie cannot hold the tension any longer, he begins to weep, tremors shudder across the wrack and ruin of his body as he forces his legs to prop it up, one hand against the side of the house.

He should run away immediately, not be seen, follow Chuck as requested. But no strength or will remain in any part or portion, all Jackie Molloy can do is breathe.

He decides that as soon as he can walk, he will go straight to the girl, somehow find her tonight, Chuck is probably doing the same thing. Jackie will get there first. To report Anna and Marilyn's failure, his own success. He no longer cares what happens to Chuck, he only wants to fall on his knees again and kiss the earth, if there is a God to thank I flood this barren land with thanks.

For Jackie believes – oh the mystery of what a mind can manufacture – that he and the girl have been spared.

38 S

Ligature strangulation – pressure on neck applied by a constricting band pulled tight by force – results in closure of blood vessels and air passages of neck

Death caused by compression/blockage of vessels supplying blood (oxygen) to brain – pressure on carotid arteries leads to loss of consciousness in 10–15 seconds. Eleven pounds of pressure needed on carotids, 4.4 on jugulars

Face and neck grossly congested, puffy, balloonlike – eyes, conjunctival tissue, and ears haemorrhage – facial blood vessels, vessels of eyelids and lips rupture (leaving red blotches on skin called 'petechiae') – Also, skin turns blue (cyanosis), especially in head and neck area – possible pink teeth due to presence of blood saturated with carbon dioxide

Haemorrhages into neck muscle; fractures of hyoid bone and thyroid cartilage

Ligature mark usually encircles neck in horizontal plane, overlies larynx or upper trachea – elevation of larynx and tongue result, air passage at level of pharynx is closed – teeth dig into tongue – difficult to block airway at level of larynx and trachea because these cartilages are tough, rigid – assailant must use extreme force

If ligature left on after death or has rubbed neck during assault, mark underneath will be a brownish, dried, leathery band – possibly deeply sunk into skin, depending on degree of force – with belt, might also be mark from buckle – but usually strangulation happens too quickly (assailant loops ligature around neck several times rapidly, tucks end under and pulls, doesn't take time to fasten buckle) – gashes from fingernails, bruises from hands, in neck area as victim struggles to remove belt

Summary

1. Increased efforts to breathe, with facial congestion and commencing cyanosis
2. Deep laboured respirations, with a heaving chest if free to move; deepened cyanosis and congestion
3. Loss of consciousness, convulsions, evacuation of bladder and bowel, vomiting. Haemmhorraging and rupture of blood vessels
4. Respirations become shallow and cease, pupils dilate and death ensues – mouth and eyes may be locked open in final attempts to breathe
5. Death can occur suddenly at any time from cardiac arrest (impaired return of blood from head to heart)

39

What more can be asked of butterflies? Of moonlight, reflecting pools, leaf-stalks or air? Have they not done enough?

Miguelito braces Jackie as he heaves to the side of the mattress. Expelling a bolus of putrid relics, thirty-five years, sixty, infinity. Parasites. Jackie Molloy laid waste.

Miguelito spreads the dripping sodden rot across his palms. The sum total as it leaks through his fingers. What of his own future?

Tomas stands, regards. No attempt to clean, oh no, do not cover disarray. Possibility possibility, stay the final note, the last to go is sound. Hear the pardon in laying bare offence. In looking.

Oh Miguelito you are next, who can bear, and on his knees the young man cries out

Please

And the old man, second chance, cries back

Acknowledgements

My daughter Annie remains until the end of time one of the great creations of the universe, a font of inspiration and wisdom, a monument to the endurance of the human spirit.

Thanks to my faithful dog, Rosie, for being there when I needed her most, across the long hours of a writer's life.

I am very grateful to my agent, Anthony Goff, of David Higham Associates, and to Carole Welch, Publisher of Sceptre Books, for their belief and patience throughout.

My thanks, too, to my brother, whose gentle words of wisdom along the way greatly eased the journey.

And always to Ailbhe Alvey for an abundance of gifts so freely given, which at every stage have made this book possible.

My writing group are a constant source of support. Again and again I thank Renate Ahrens-Kramer, Julie Parsons, Sheila Barrett, Phil MacCarthy, Cecelia McGovern, and Joan O'Neill.

I am indebted beyond words to Renate Ahrens-Kramer for her staunch commitment to me and my work at every turn on the hazardous journey, and deeply thankful to Julie Parsons whose exceptional generosity of friendship, insight, and unflinching honesty have had a profound impact on this book.

How can I ever express my gratitude for the sustaining

presence of my mother and father, without whom I could not have dreamt of completing this book.

Louisburgh, Co. Mayo
August 1996